BEEN HERE ALL ALONG

Sandy Hall

A Swoon Reads Book
An imprint of Macmillan Publishers Limited

First published in the US 2016 by Swoon Reads, an imprint of Feiwel and Friends

First published in the UK 2017 by Macmillan Children's Books
an imprint of Pan Macmillan
20 New Wharf Road, London N1 9RR
Associated companies throughout the world
www.panmacmillan.com

ISBN 978-1-5098-5280-2

1 3 5 7 9 8 6 4 2

A CIP catalogue record for this book is available from
the British Library.

Book design by Ashley Halsey
Printed and bound by CPI Group (UK) Ltd, Croydon CR0 4YY

For Holly West, without whom this book,
and so many others, would not exist.

PROLOGUE
Twelve Years Earlier

Ezra

Like a hundred years ago my mom asked me to watch my five-year-old brother Gideon while he played in the backyard. But then I got bored, because he's a boring kid, and now I realize he's not actually in the backyard anymore.

I need to find that little a-hole before my mom notices and I get in trouble for him going missing or whatever.

I can't yell for him, though, and I can't let my mom notice that I can't find him, so I need to be super stealth about it. Like a ninja. On the other hand, if she comes outside and doesn't see him, I can just say that we're playing hide-and-seek. It's good to have a plan.

I tiptoe around the yard, whispering his name.

I finally find him, all the way behind the garage, where he's not supposed to play because it's so close to the woods and the highway behind the woods. Our dad says they need to build a wall by the highway, but they haven't yet. That's why Gideon isn't allowed back there. I'm technically not allowed back there either. But I'm almost eleven, and I make my own decisions.

"You're not supposed to be back here," I say when I find him. He's playing in the dirt with some tiny little blond kid who looks at me like I'm trying to kidnap him or something.

"I made a friend," Gideon says, pointing at the blond kid.

The kid stands up and stares at me.

"What's his name?" I ask. Maybe Gideon found a runaway. Maybe there's a huge reward for this kid. Gideon's young and dumb and I could keep most of the money and just buy him some toys. He'd never know the difference.

"He didn't tell me," Gideon says as he stands up. He takes the other boy's hand protectively.

"Are you lost?" I ask him.

He squeezes Gideon's hand and shakes his head. He points toward the house next door.

"Did you just move here?" I ask.

He nods a whole bunch of times in a row.

"You should go home," I tell him.

His eyes go wide and he runs in the direction of his house, which probably seems a lot farther away than it really is, since the kid's so tiny.

"Good-bye, new friend!" Gideon yells after him, waving.

"I'm gonna tell Mom that you were behind the garage and she's gonna be so pissed at you!" I tell Gideon as we walk toward the house.

"I'm gonna tell Mom you said a bad word," Gideon answers. He's too smart for a five-year-old.

one

Gideon

Football players.

Cheerleaders.

Basketball players, when they make the state championships.

Maybe people in the marching band?

I'm trying to make a list of people who actually enjoy pep rallies while I'm getting ready for school. It seems like a limited portion of the population. Because let me tell you, as someone who's always sitting in the bleachers during pep rallies, they are probably the most boring things on the face of the planet. I'd rather watch golf.

I definitely never feel the proper level of pep while I sit there. It's just people hopping around on the gym floor. I don't even know what they're doing, or what it's supposed to look like. It really just seems like everyone is bouncing up and down and trying to get me to bounce up and down.

I have zero desire to bounce.

I also dislike clapping. What are we, trained seals?

I have far better things to do with my life than deal with any of this. But apparently having certain aspirations does not preclude me from having to attend another pep rally. My request to use the wasteful pep rally time to study SAT vocabulary was quickly shot down by the vice principal. Doesn't mean I'm not going to have a pile of flash cards in my pocket. The administration can't stop me from becoming more than my monosyllabic classmates could ever imagine.

For the record, I'm self-aware enough to realize my biggest issue with pep rallies is that they bring into harsh focus what a complete nerd I am. But I don't need to spread that around to anyone.

As I walk into the kitchen, my mother's pouring herself a cup of coffee.

"Pour me one, too," I say.

"For starters, please or thank you goes a long way. And since when do you drink coffee?" She continues preparing her own cup with plenty of cream and sugar.

"Since forever," I say, getting out my own mug, since she's obviously not going to be any help in this matter.

She leans a hip on the counter and stares me down. "You need a haircut."

"My hair is fine, Ma." I put a piece of bread in the toaster.

"And coffee stunts your growth."

"Thank you for bringing the topic of my height up at 7:07 in the morning. It's never too early to remind me that I'm Lilliputian." I pour some coffee from the carafe and drink it black, as if trying to prove my virility and manliness via coffee preferences.

"I'm not trying to make you feel bad!" she insists. "I'm your mother. I know you want to be tall. You want to be at least as tall as Ezra."

"Ezra's only five-ten," I point out, gesturing toward her with my mug and then taking a sip, wincing a bit and giving in to the call of cream and sugar.

"And how tall are you these days?" she asks, eyeing me up.

"Five-seven," I say. "Almost."

"Just think how much taller you would be if you didn't drink coffee."

"I really don't think it works like that."

"But what if it does, Gideon? What if it really does and you're harming yourself?"

I roll my eyes and sigh deeply. I chug the rest of my coffee and shove toast in my mouth while she nags me for a few more minutes, then put my mug in the dishwasher and run back upstairs to brush my teeth.

"Gideon," she calls after me.

"Can't now, Ma, Kyle's gonna be ready to go any second."

As soon as I say his name, I start thinking again about the pep rally. I need to find out if he actually likes them. Maybe Kyle is the key to the mystery of pep rallies.

He plays center for the varsity basketball team. My mom always says that Kyle's like a puppy that's still growing into his paws. Which is probably true but a weird thing to agree with your mom about in terms of your best friend.

I should have pointed out to her that Kyle drinks coffee sometimes and he's six-three.

Because of his height, he spends a lot of time hunched over and brushing his hair away from his ears, trying to hear what all the tiny peasants around him are saying.

I just can't imagine that he really enjoys this clichéd high school ritual. I can already see him standing in the middle of the basketball court, trying not to call too much attention to himself, while the cheerleaders and the rest of the team draw everyone's focus.

Kyle definitely prefers the simpler things in life. Sports, video games, Lord of the Rings, even though I keep telling him he can't be a true Tolkien fan without reading the books. He pretends he can't hear me when I say stuff like that.

I think he's one of those guys who is really lucky because he's quiet, but instead of people thinking that he's an aloof weirdo, people find him sort of charming. He's not as quiet as he used to be. When I first met him when we were five, he was so quiet I didn't know his name until his mom told me.

As I head back downstairs to leave, my mom's gathering up her stuff by the front door to leave for a meeting.

"You know," I say, "Kyle's six-three and he drinks coffee."

"Maybe Kyle comes from a stronger gene pool."

"Do you just stay up all night thinking about ways to make me feel bad?" I ask.

"Don't be a smart aleck. I love you," she says, then kisses me on the forehead, leaving a lipstick stain for sure. I dart out of the way before she decides to do something gross like lick her thumb and clean off my forehead.

"Be a good boy, Gideon."

"See you later, Ma," I say, closing the door and rubbing at the lipstick with my own spitless thumb.

Kyle

I'm definitely running late.

Up until I was about ten, I firmly believed there were little elves that came into my room every night and rearranged all my stuff. At seventeen, I realize that's not how it works, but it doesn't keep me from wishing that there really were little elves, because it'd be nice to have someone else to blame. The reality is that I'm extremely disorganized and forgetful.

Finding all the stuff I need for school every morning takes up a solid half hour of time. I have no idea why. I try to do better and yet here I am, running around the house looking for my basketball jersey that I need for this afternoon's pep rally.

I don't even like pep rallies.

Too many people looking at me.

I check all the usual places for my jersey: my bedroom, the downstairs bathroom, the upstairs bathroom, the linen closet, just in case. I systematically check all of my dresser drawers. But nothing. My mom set up all these cubbies and color-coded systems and foolproof ways to keep everything I need exactly where I leave it. Unfortunately, I am a fool.

I'm an especially tired fool because I kept myself up half the night worrying about coming out as bi to my girlfriend.

But that's a whole other circle of thoughts that I don't have time to get into at the moment.

I need my damn basketball jersey.

"Mom!" I yell, finally giving in.

"Mom!" I call again as I run down the stairs. I check the clock on the cable box as I breeze through the living room. It's already 7:17. I have three minutes until Gideon's going to be standing outside, waiting for me. Gideon is never late. Gideon never loses anything. Ever.

I guess that's just what his parents expect from him. Although I've known the Berkos since I was five, and they've never struck me as the kind of parents who would force their kid to be something he's not, and yet Gideon is a model son.

But you should see Gideon's older brother, Ezra. He's got the raddest freaking tattoos all over his body, and instead of going to college, he decided to move to California and become a professional surfer. I honestly can't think of anything cooler than that. Or any one human being more opposite to Gideon.

And on top of that, the Berkos were totally cool about it. And actually supportive. I feel like if I proposed that to my parents, they would basically lock me in my room for the next four years and force me to get an online degree. After the online degree, they would probably let me do whatever I wanted, but they're super into going to college. I think because they didn't go themselves.

"Mom!" I yell again. "Mom! Mom!"

"What, what, what?" she asks, coming up from the basement with my basketball jersey in hand.

"I was looking for that!" I say, grabbing it from her.

"I washed it for you. I told you I was washing it for you."

"Oh."

"Now eat something before you're late."

I look over at the breakfast table, where my sisters are eating bowls of cereal and being complete opposites as usual. Julie is typing furiously on her phone while Emma looks about half-asleep.

"And you two need to get out to the bus," she adds, staring them down.

My mom works in an office that she loves doing a job that she hates, but she doesn't have to be there until nine, so she's still wandering around the house in her pajamas, yelling at us. It's not until my sisters leave for the bus to the middle school that she goes upstairs to get ready herself and I'm left in peace and quiet for the ninety seconds it takes me to eat a Pop-Tart, brush my teeth, and grab the rest of my stuff.

"See you later, Mom!" I yell up the stairs. I get a muffled reply as I turn to walk out the door, but a second later she's at the top of the stairs.

"Hold on," she says.

I freeze, trying to remember what I'm in trouble for.

"Gideon's gonna kill me if I'm late," I say, glancing toward the living room again, but I can't see the digital clock on the cable box anymore.

"Are you going to be home for dinner?" she asks.

"I'm supposed to hang out with Ruby after basketball practice."

She sighs that kind of put-upon mom sigh that I know too well. I haven't been home for dinner much lately.

"But for you, Mom, I'll make an exception."

She rolls her eyes but smiles. "All right, get out of here before Gideon calls in the SWAT team."

When I get outside, Gideon's leaning on my car, checking his watch like it holds the secrets of the universe.

I'm about to apologize when he starts talking.

"Do you like pep rallies?" he asks.

"I can't stand them," I tell him honestly, shuddering a little at the very thought.

"Awesome," he says, climbing into the passenger side.

"You have lipstick on your forehead."

"Damn it," Gideon says, pulling down the visor and checking himself in the mirror.

"Should be a napkin in the glove compartment," I say.

He roots around in there while I pull out of the driveway and head in the direction of the Dunkin' Donuts drive-through.

"So, what's up?" he asks.

"Nothing."

"Why were you running late?"

I shrug.

"No, really, you seem weird," he says, side-eying me. "You're all twitchy."

"Um, well. I think I'm going to come out to Ruby."

"What? Seriously? Why?"

"Well, um . . ." I can't find my train of thought, and I have no idea why I'm so nervous.

"I mean, like, why now? What changed?"

"It kind of feels like I'm lying to her."

"But you like girls. Like, how relevant is this? What guys do you even like?"

"Chris Evans," I say.

He rolls his eyes. "Barring the unlikely event that you happen to run into Chris Evans, how big of a role does being bisexual really play in your everyday life?"

"Why are you acting like this?"

"Like what?" he asks.

"Like I'm on trial for wanting to come out to my girlfriend."

His jaw drops as he realizes that's exactly how he's acting.

"Is it because you're one of those people who don't believe bisexuality exists or something?" I ask.

"Hell no."

"Then what?"

"I don't know, it's one of those things where I know I'm acting weird but I can't get myself to stop. I'll do better. I promise."

"Good."

"So how do you think she'll take it?" he asks, holding on to the "oh shit" handle for dear life as I take a curve a little too fast.

"Hopefully she'll be cool about it. I don't think she'll assume it means we should have a threesome or something."

"Who did you come out to that asked you to have a three-some?"

"No one. But think about it. It's got to happen all the time. 'Oh, you swing both ways? Let's invite a second dude into our ménage.'"

"Exactly how much porn have you been watching lately, Kyle?" he asks, his face mock serious.

"There is nothing wrong with porn," I say, wrenching the steering wheel in the other direction.

"I didn't say there was, just that you might be watching too much of it."

I roll my eyes.

"Just so I'm up on all of this, who knows you're bi?"

"Pretty much my whole family except for my great-aunt Alba, but that's just because she's senile, you, your parents, your brother, Buster, Sawyer, and Maddie. Why, did you hear something?"

"Nope. But who's going to gossip about you to me?"

"An excellent point."

"I guess what I don't understand is why you seem nervous about coming out to her when so many people already know."

"Another excellent point." I chew my lip. "I guess it's just different with Ruby because, I don't know, she might not like me as much after she knows. Or something."

"If that's the case, then she's basically just an asshole."

"I know."

I make a sharp left into the Dunkin' Donuts parking lot and gun the engine toward the drive-through.

"You could warn a guy," Gideon says, rubbing his throat where the seat belt cut into his neck.

"Hey, Gideon, we're going to Dunkin' Donuts," I say.

"Thanks for the heads-up," he says.

"I had a Lord of the Rings marathon last night," I tell him after I place our order.

"Is that why you were actually running late?"

"Um, maybe," I say.

"You watched without me? I thought we were saving it for spring break."

"Well, we were, but I don't know, I couldn't sleep. I was thinking too much about coming out to Ruby. I only watched the first two and not the extended editions!"

"Oh," he says, his voice quiet.

"Anyway, I was thinking—"

"We're not having the conversation about the eagles again. We're not going down that road. Our friendship cannot withstand that debate."

"I'm not talking about that," I say, trying to get him to listen.

"Good. I'm not prepared for that debate at 7:32 in the morning."

"I'm mostly just wondering what would happen if someone swallowed the ring," I say when I finally park the car on the side street next to the high school.

"Why would anyone swallow the ring?" he asks.

"I don't know. But hypothetically, what do you think would happen?"

Gideon shakes his head and continues walking toward the front doors.

"No, but really, Gid, come on. I thought we could have a nice conversation about this!" I call after him.

"It's not going to end well," he says over his shoulder as I catch up.

"But just think about it."

He rolls his eyes, but I can tell he's going to think about it. This is how it is, was, and always will be between Gideon and me.

two

Ruby

I don't really understand why people hate pep rallies.

I'm head cheerleader. I probably love them by default. There's a semi-decent chance that I'm biased about the whole thing. But really, what's not to like?

People are so anti-pep that the administration had to move all pep rallies to the middle of the day so that everyone would stop cutting them at the end of the day.

I mean, I guess it's always nice to get out of school early. Maybe if I didn't have to cheer during them, I'd want to leave, too.

But what I really don't understand is why Gideon Berko is currently sitting in the bleachers going over flash cards. Probably SAT vocabulary.

Instead of trying to understand him, I just clap my hands and shake my pom-poms even harder. It's the least I can do for Kyle, who's so bashful during these things it makes me want to prod him out into the spotlight. His hands are shoved deep into his pockets, and he's shaking his head just the right way so his hair falls in his eyes. But he's smiling. He can't hide the fact that he's smiling.

He's a good boyfriend. An amazing one, even. Probably the best I've ever had, because I don't think he's dating me just to be able to say that he's dating a cheerleader.

I thought for sure my senior year would be completely boring and devoid of fun. Until Kyle showed up, looking adorable and nervous as he approached me at the homecoming dance back in October. For once there was a guy who liked me who didn't say all the right things.

I'd be lying if I said I'd never noticed him before. It was hard to miss him when he was a sophomore playing starting center. He made a pretty big splash for a kid who up to that point seemed to have only one friend.

When the pep rally finally ends, I help the other girls clean up some of the posters and confetti. I spot Kyle and Gideon leaving the room together. They're like magnets. They will find each other anywhere, anytime.

After they're gone, I think about how other people look at them. People who don't know them. But it's hard, now that I've spent time with Kyle and Gideon, to look at them the same way I used to.

I used to think they were just really big nerds.

Looking back, though, I also remember seeing them

laughing all the time. Like they were sharing the best jokes that the world has ever known. They didn't actually care if I was sitting across the cafeteria from them, thinking that they were nerds. It didn't keep them from passing notes in Elvish.

It still doesn't keep them from doing that, no matter how many times I've joked about being uncomfortable that they're talking shit about me in a made-up language. Kyle insists that they're not saying anything bad. But he never actually says they're not talking about me.

But as Kyle is so quick to remind me, not *everything* is about me.

I like to tell him that it should be. And I'm only joking a little bit when I say it.

Kyle

I think the new English teacher is out to get me or something. Mrs. Masterson, my old teacher, who was really, really, really old, freaking loved me. She knew I was smart and she didn't pressure me. I'd had her for English since freshman year, and she let certain things slide. Like how bad my spelling is or when I couldn't make the right connections between characters while we were reading *The Crucible*.

But we only read two or three books a year with her. It helped that she would read most of them to us in class, because I don't think she knew what else to do with the time. Also she'd read us a lot of poetry. She was really into poetry.

During winter break she fell on some ice and broke her hip. I guess that made her realize how old she was, so she decided to retire. Now I have this new teacher for English, Ms. Gupta, who's trying too hard to connect with everyone.

We started on a Shakespeare unit in January. Our first play was *King Lear*, and I just didn't get it. None of it made sense to me. Sometimes she'd give people parts to read out loud. That's when she noticed how much trouble I have with reading. I just couldn't keep up. My hands got all sweaty and the words started to blur. The worst part was how quiet everyone else got around me while I tried to push through one stupid sentence.

We're juniors in high school. We should never be forced to read aloud in class. I can read fine to myself when I can go slowly. I'm just really bad at not getting nervous and stumbling and I take a long time. Everyone gets bored listening to me.

And in elementary school I used to get made fun of because I was so bad at reading. That doesn't help. That doesn't make you a very confident reader later in life. But that shouldn't make or break my English grade ten years later.

After the *King Lear* incident, she started calling on me more, and then she started asking me to stay after class.

So for the past three months she's been trying to "work with" me because apparently in her world I'm close to failing English, even though I always got a C+ from Mrs. Masterson. But since it was the last class of the day and I had basketball practice, there hasn't really been time to talk.

Unfortunately, today all the class periods were a couple of minutes shorter to make room for the pep rally earlier, so when the bell rings, it kind of throws me off. I'm usually ready to sprint out of this classroom in fear that Ms. Gupta is going to want to talk. She catches me, of course, since I'm one of the last people walking out of the room.

"Kyle?" she calls out. She has a nice voice. I really like it, actually. It's got just this little hint of an Indian accent, and she sounds all smooth and smart.

"I don't wanna be late for practice," I say, just barely turning around.

"I know, I know. Big game coming up. But just one second."

I turn fully around and make sure I don't meet her eye. I'm playing cool, pretending to be a tree. That usually works pretty well for me.

"Yeah, can't disappoint the team," I say, when she fails to continue. I sneak a glance at her desk and notice she's going through some papers. Probably the essays we handed in last week.

She grimaces and shows me the 60 percent on the top of my paper. "Did you understand any of the instructions?"

I take the essay from her and look at all the red slashes through words and sentences, different call-outs that I can't actually read right now because my brain is so foggy and nervous.

I hand it back to her and squeeze the straps of my backpack. "I worked really hard," I finally say. I sound so whiny.

"I think there's more to it than just needing to work hard. Some of this is—" She pauses, skimming the page again. "You have moments where I can see how smart you are, and there are other sentences where you obviously let spell-check change every word and it turned into gibberish."

"Spelling is, like, not my best." My tongue is heavy in my mouth and my brain is working in slow motion so I can't even think of the right words.

"It's not just the spelling, though. It's the context and comprehension. There's so much more going on here."

I know she's trying to make eye contact with me, like we're supposed to be having some kind of moment. But I can't. I stare outside and watch a squirrel hop around in a tree. I wouldn't mind going out there and joining him. Maybe just live in that tree for the rest of my life and learn English through the classroom window.

"I really don't want you to fail this marking period. Grades are due next week, and you're right on the cusp. An F isn't going to look great on your report card."

"I know," I say, still watching the little squirrel.

"It could mean summer school if you don't pull it together."

I wince at the idea of more school. Especially since I found out last week I got accepted into a really prestigious basketball camp for this summer.

She gives me detailed instructions about what she wants me to do for extra credit, and I make sure I write everything down. I really don't want to have to worry about this.

"I believe you're a very smart kid who's having some problems," she says after the world's longest instructions. "We will be able to come up with a solution. You are not a lost cause. I checked your grades, and I see you've done just fine in the past."

"Yeah, Mrs. Masterson was a good teacher."

She nods distractedly. "I have to wonder if there's something else going on."

"Something else?" I ask.

"A personal problem, maybe? I'm not trying to pry. I want to understand what changed. It might help me."

"No," I say. "Nothing changed."

"Everything's good at home?"

I nod and wipe my forehead. I feel sweaty and nervous and like I can't focus on anything.

"Okay, well," she says.

I take that as the opportunity to leave without saying another word, because there's nothing else to say.

The halls are almost clear by the time I get to my locker, and Ruby's leaning on it, waiting for me.

"You okay?" she asks.

I blink hard. "Uh, yeah. I just had to stay and talk to Ms. Gupta for a second."

"Oh, cool. I love her. Such a step up from Old Lady Masterson. That woman did not like me."

I nod but decide to drop the topic while I grab what I need from my locker, and then I'm ready to go.

"You're really okay?" she asks as we turn down the hallway in the direction of the gym.

"Yeah, fine, just a lot on my mind." We pause outside the locker rooms before parting ways. "I know we were supposed to go out tonight after practice, but I have to go home. My mom's on my ass about never being home for dinner."

"Oh no, a nice home-cooked meal! That sounds terrible!" she says.

"You want to come over?" I ask, sort of hoping she'll say no. I have too much to think about. For starters, I need to work on this extra-credit thing for English.

"Nah, I think I'll skip this round of family fun time at the Kaminskys'."

"Figured it was worth asking."

"Thanks," she says.

"See you after practice," I say.

She kisses my cheek and turns to walk away, but I grab her hand, pulling her back. I kiss her harder and longer than I normally would in the middle of the hallway at school. But it just feels kind of right.

"Such an animal, Kaminsky. I like it," she says.

I can't help but smile.

Ruby

By the time we're both done, it's getting dark outside and I don't really feel like dredging up whatever was making Kyle nervous earlier. When I meet up with him outside the gym, instead I lean up to kiss him on the cheek.

"You smell like sweaty boy," I say.

"Well, probably because I am a sweaty boy."

"So sassy lately, Kaminsky," I say, swinging our hands between us as we walk out to his car.

"Why do you like me?" he asks a few minutes later as we pull out of the school parking lot.

I study his profile in the flitting glow of the passing street-lights.

I try to think of an exact reason, to pinpoint something

that doesn't sound flimsy or trite. Because I like him for all those reasons you're supposed to like people. He's kind and warm and looks at me like I'm the coolest bitch on earth. And I am. But there's more to it.

"You don't have to answer that," he mumbles after I've been quiet for too long. "It's not important."

"I think part of why I like you is that you ask questions like that," I finally say.

He licks his lips, waiting for me to go on, but when I don't, he babbles. "But why? Like, that doesn't really tell me anything. We've been together for six months and I've seen the way other guys look at you. You could have pretty much any of them."

"I like that you gave me a chance."

We're at my house by now and he pulls over, shutting off the car. "I gave you a chance?" he asks, turning fully to look at me.

"Yeah, you know. You don't talk to a lot of girls, but you talked to me. I didn't expect it. It made me feel special or something stupid like that." God, this is too hard to talk about for some reason. I don't think I like this emotional crap.

"So if I tell you something kind of personal, and sort of weird, you'll still like me?" he asks.

"Of course," I say, my voice quiet, remembering his discomfort earlier.

"So I'm bi," he says.

"Huh?"

"Bi."

"Are you telling me to leave?"

"What? No. I'm bisexual."

"Cool," I say.

"Cool?"

"Yeah, of course. I don't know what you want me to say, but that's cool. I'm cool with that."

He rolls his neck and it cracks like a gunshot.

"So you were a little nervous about telling me that?" I ask, taking his chin in my hand and turning him toward me.

"I was. I don't tell a lot of people, but we're just, we've been getting closer? I felt like you should know or else it, you know, it felt like I was lying. And I really don't want to lie to anyone, but especially not you and—"

My mouth is on his, and it drowns out whatever other useless words were trying to claw their way out of his throat. He doesn't need to make excuses or overexplain with me. I hope he understands that.

His phone buzzes, and he leans his forehead on mine.

"That's definitely my mom. And I definitely need to go home."

"It's cool. We have a date this weekend anyway."

"Oh yeah, the dance," he says.

"Hopefully it'll be a victory dance when you guys win tomorrow night," I say, the cheerleader in me leaking out of my pores.

"Yeah, it should be fun."

I look right at him, forcing his eyes to meet mine in the dim light. "Thanks for coming out to me."

"You're welcome."

I slide out of the car and run up the steps to my house, turning back to wave.

He always waits to make sure I'm safe.

Just one more reason to like him.

three

Kyle

Ruby and I walk into the gym like we own the place.

The basketball team won the state championships last night, so this dance feels like a serious victory lap.

She takes my hand and we do a circuit of the gym, where she says hello to people and I try to get a better look at the refreshments while fist-bumping and high-fiving people I'm not sure I've ever seen before. Do they even go to this school?

But there are leaf cookies on that table, and I want to eat all the pink ones. Ruby seems to be ignoring my soulful eye contact with the cookie table.

"Come on, let's slow dance," she says, yanking me toward the front of the gym, where a bunch of couples sway to a song that sounds like a slow love ballad, but if you listen closely to the lyrics, it really isn't romantic. After threading our way through the crowd, she stops suddenly and turns, throwing her hands around my neck middle-school style.

"Kyle," Ruby says in a singsong voice, "what are you thinking about?"

I only half hear her because I see someone make a move toward my cookies.

"God you're cute when you're barely listening to me."

"Huh?" I say, hunching over to hear her better.

"You're cute," she stage-whispers.

I smile.

"Aren't I cute?"

"You're better than cute," I say. "You look awesome tonight, by the way, in case I haven't mentioned it."

"Thanks." She takes a deep breath and it's like every hair on my body stands up. Like I have a sixth sense that she's about to start a fight. "I don't want this to be a *thing* or whatever, but now that you've gotten through the big game, I just have a question."

"Okay," I say.

"How come you waited so long to tell me you were bi?"

That gets my attention away from the cookies. I blink at her, unsure of how to respond.

"I'm not offended, I just"—she pauses and cocks her head to the side—"I guess I don't understand why you waited until we were together for six months to tell me."

I raise my eyebrows and open my mouth to say something,

anything, because it seems like she's asking questions but they're also statements. She keeps talking before I can figure out what to say again.

"Really, it's not a big deal, but I kind of can't shake the feeling that you don't actually trust me."

I stop dancing and step back from her. "Would you rather I hadn't told you?"

"No. That's not what I'm saying at all. I guess I don't understand why you decided to tell me now."

"Because it's my choice when to tell someone personal things about me."

"But I'm your girlfriend."

"And that means you should know everything right away?"

"No, but I should know stuff like this before other people."

I cross my arms. "What's that supposed to mean?"

"Like, when did you tell Gideon?"

"I don't know. A long time ago. But Gideon's been my best friend since before kindergarten. Of course I would have told him."

"So you've known the whole time we've been going out?"

"Yes."

"And you never wanted to tell me before?" she asks, throwing up her hands in exasperation. She pulls away from me and walks off the dance floor. I catch up to her right by the refreshment table.

"I did, it just makes me really nervous," I explain, hoping she'll get it. "Does it change something for you? Do you not like me anymore or something?"

"No. I still like you. I hate to sound like a broken record, but I don't understand why you wanted to tell me now. Why not sooner?"

She stares up at me, and I get the terrible feeling like she might cry. She chews on the inside of her lip, like she's just barely holding back her tears.

"I'm sorry if I hurt your feelings by not telling you sooner," I say. It's the best I can do in that moment, because the whole situation boggles my mind.

"I know you said in the car that it was because you felt closer lately, but haven't we always been close? I'm your girl-friend."

"Yes, you are. I guess I don't know what to say to you to make this better."

"I just, I need a couple minutes," she says, sniffling. She spins on her heel and speed-walks away. I'm left standing there by the refreshment table with my mouth hanging open.

And there's only one broken pink leaf cookie left.

Isn't that just the way life is sometimes?

Gideon

I sit up in the balcony completely stunned, watching the whole thing go down between Kyle and Ruby. I've never seen them so much as frown at each other before, but this is something different. This is an actual fight. Even from far away, I can tell that something is really wrong.

I don't know what Kyle's face looked like, because he had his back to me the whole time, but Ruby's was like a slide show of different kinds of emotions. Sad, angry, frustrated, very sad—it kept getting worse and worse.

You hear the phrase all the time, that someone raised their hackles, but I don't think I've ever seen it to actually identify the action. As Kyle stood there, his whole back, shoulders, and neck tensed up. It should have been hard to watch. But I couldn't look away.

I'm hanging out with my friends Maddie and Sawyer, the ultimate power couple of class politics, but they're totally unaware of the drama unfolding below. I'm glad neither of them notices that I completely checked out of the conversation several minutes ago.

I should stop watching. Their fight is none of my business. I know it, but I can't stop staring. I must sit there with my mouth hanging open for a good five minutes. I feel something welling up in my chest. It's something like hope, but I don't know why. And it makes me want to laugh for some reason, to the point where I have to put my hand over my mouth.

"You okay?" Sawyer asks, nudging my arm.

"Yeah, what's up? You're awfully quiet," Maddie says.

A couple of Kyle's basketball friends are hanging out behind us. I had situated my little group that way in hope that Kyle would notice and come hang out up here. But now that Ruby stormed away and he's making his way toward the balcony, I don't think I can talk to him without either laughing in his face or asking way too many questions about what happened with Ruby.

I make a quick excuse and exit the bleachers as fast as possible.

I make a beeline for the boys' locker room. No one's in

there, thank God. The last thing I need is to be harassed by a bunch of jocks while my emotions are going haywire.

"Why did I feel like laughing?" I ask the empty room. Row upon row of green lockers stare back at me like soldiers standing in formation. I'm definitely losing my mind, because it feels like they're judging me. "Why did watching Kyle and Ruby fight make me want to laugh?

"Do I like Ruby?" I ask the lockers, as I walk toward the sinks. "Do I have feelings for her?" I stand there in the empty locker room and think about Ruby. Her hair is nice. Long, dark, and shiny, all those things shampoo commercials tell you are important. I think about kissing Ruby.

"No. I don't like Ruby," I say.

I wash my face and try to make sense of what I'm feeling. I slump onto a bench and lean my head against the wall, closing my eyes and covering my face with my hands.

"What is wrong with me?" Again I find myself talking out loud to no one.

I rub my eyes and turn my head to the left. There on the window of the coach's office is a posed photo of this year's basketball team.

Kyle stands in the center of the back row. He's the only guy smiling. All the others have on these stoic, tough-guy jock faces. I can't help but smile back. I think about brushing his hair back off his forehead, which is not something I would ever do in real life, but I *think* about doing it all the time. Kyle pays better attention when his hair isn't in his way.

The Gideon in my head does something completely

unexpected then. He runs his hand down Kyle's cheek and moves it around to the back of his neck, before pulling him closer and pressing their lips together.

The Gideon sitting in the locker room suddenly can't breathe.

All the air is gone from my lungs. Is this what a panic attack feels like?

I take a few deep breaths and try to calm down. I've heard that if you can talk, you can breathe, so I say out loud, "Why would I be thinking about kissing Kyle?"

Paranoia sets in immediately that while I was panicking, someone came in and might have heard me, so I take a quick circle around the locker room and make sure I really am alone.

I sink back down onto the bench when I'm positive that no one is in here with me. I've worked hard to never deal with these kinds of feelings. I decided a long time ago that I'd figure out dating and girls in college. I don't have time for that stuff if I want to get into a good school.

This is not part of the plan.

But maybe I didn't have time for girls because I don't *like* girls.

I think I might pass out. I'm sweating, my hands are shaking, my eyes are blurry. Maybe I'm getting sick. Or maybe I like Kyle and have repressed it so hard for so long that acknowledging it now has forced me to the brink of sanity.

Am I gay or do I just like Kyle? 'Cause if I just like Kyle, then maybe I'm bi? Or pan or one of those other spectrum-y things? Could I possibly just be Kyle-sexual? Is that a thing?

I take a deep breath and count to ten. That's supposed to be soothing, right?

Then I start trying to think of an SAT vocabulary word for each letter of the alphabet. I love vocabulary words.

After about ten minutes, I stand up and face my reflection in the mirror. I hold myself tall, squaring my shoulders, and look myself in the eye. I take a deep breath, pulling air all the way into my lungs and taking a long time to blow it out again.

I feel better, less panicked, but I have some things to think about.

Kyle

I'm still stunned as I head up the stairs to the balcony, taking them two at a time to distance myself from what happened with Ruby out in the middle of the gym. If anyone saw it, then that means *everyone* will be talking about it soon enough. I really hope no one could hear the specifics. I'm not sure if I'm ready for everyone in school to know I'm bi.

I see Sawyer and Maddie first and walk over to them, figuring Gideon must be somewhere nearby.

"Have you guys seen Gideon?" I ask, leaning against the railing. I notice Buster and McKinley and a couple of other guys from the team are a row up the bleachers. I lean over to them and we slap hands. I'll go sit there as soon as I figure out where Gid is.

"He ran off a minute ago," Sawyer says, looking in the direction of the stairs I just came up.

"He looked kind of, I don't know, sick to his stomach," Maddie says, making a face.

"Is he coming back?" I ask. "I was supposed to drive him home later."

Maddie shrugs. "He didn't say. He just booked it out of here."

I nod and then hop up the bleachers to sit with the guys on the team, half waiting for Gideon to come back and half wishing I was still talking to Sawyer and Maddie. Because even though I think of them as Gideon's friends, they feel more like my people than a lot of these guys do. Except for Buster. Buster is totally my bro. He just gets me. I think because I was there when he got his nickname busting his hand while trying to karate chop a cinder block.

I lean my elbows back on the row behind me, close my eyes, and zone out for a while, imagining Ruby's friends, and my friends, and Gideon's friends doing something together.

But even just thinking about her makes me feel terrible. I feel shitty for making her feel like I don't trust her, but I don't like the fact that because I took my time coming out to her, she's turned it around to mean something completely different. It's a whole confusing circular issue, and I don't know how to fix it.

Gideon sits down next to me just as I'm thinking that maybe I should go home.

"Hey," I say, sitting up and turning toward him.

"Hey," he says.

"Are you sick or something?"

"No. I'm fine."

He doesn't look fine, not at all. He looks kind of sweaty and confused.

"Just don't throw up on me," I say.

"I'm not gonna throw up on you," he says.

"You threw up on me that time in third grade."

"I threw up near you, not on you."

"Same difference. There was a splash zone," I say. "But seriously, if you feel sick, we should get out of here. I don't mind leaving early."

"You don't?" he asks, his expression doubtful.

"Ruby and I had a fight."

"Yeah, I saw."

"I don't know what to do."

"Apologize?"

"How do you know it was my fault?"

He gives me a knowing look.

"It really wasn't my fault, though. She's blowing the whole thing out of proportion."

"What?"

"She's upset that—" I pause, shooting a glance to see who's around us. Buster's leaning in to listen but I don't mind, so I continue. "That I didn't come out to her sooner."

Buster shakes his head. "Chicks are so sensitive."

"But it's not really her thing to be upset about," I say.

Gideon sighs. "It's not, but it's not like it has absolutely nothing to do with her. You've known for a long time. She might need a little time to adjust."

"But it's not her thing to adjust to. It's about me. It's not fair for her to be pissed about something that only concerns me."

"Maybe that's what she's pissed about, numb-nuts," Buster says from my other side. "Like, she wants you to care about what she thinks and, like, know that, I don't know, she's an important part of your life. That she's, like, concerned, too, or whatever."

"I can't believe I'm about to say this, but somewhere in there, Buster made a valid point," Gideon says.

Buster smiles like someone just gave him the Nobel Prize for Relationship Doctoring. "I am so valid," Buster says.

"Go make up with her," Gideon says, punching me in the arm and then staring at his knuckles like he just noticed they exist.

"Yes, you must go to her," Buster says like he's some kind of love guru. "It is the only way."

"All right, I'll be back to find you before we leave." I stand up and stretch.

"Nah," Gideon says. "Hang out with Ruby. I don't want you to get in even more trouble."

"Shut up, I never get in trouble."

"Sure you don't. But really, I'll get a ride home from these guys," he says, tapping Sawyer on the back.

"Cool, thanks."

I say good-bye to everyone, and as I head for the stairs I take a look behind me for a little extra reassurance, maybe a thumbs-up or something, but Gideon is watching me go with that sweaty and confused expression on his face.

Ruby

Kyle finds me outside the girls' bathroom near the senior lockers, hanging out with my friends Lilah and Lauren. I wanted to complain to them and tell them the whole story of what happened with Kyle, but it's hard because I know I shouldn't talk about his sexual preferences. That's none of their business. I get that.

But it's my business when and how he tells me things, and this just felt wrong to me when I started thinking about it too much.

I know I'm being kind of a weirdo about the whole thing, but it made me question our relationship. Not whether he likes me or not, but why he would wait to tell me. It's a gray area, though. At least, that's what I've decided. Because with a little more distance, I know I'm partially in the wrong here.

And the fact that he came looking for me makes me feel very willing to apologize.

"We're gonna go back to the dance, Ru," Lauren says when she sees Kyle. She tugs Lilah's arm to drag her along.

"Hey," he says, wiping his hands on his jeans nervously. "I just—"

"No, wait. Listen. I am so sorry. I've been thinking about it, and I overreacted. It's like sometimes I forget that I'm not the boss of the world. It's your thing to tell, and you should take your time and wait for your moment."

"Well, I'm sorry I wasn't getting what you were saying," he says. "And it is my thing to tell, thank you for saying that, but I wasn't understanding your point at all."

"I wasn't doing a good job making my point." I roll my eyes. "I get super jealous sometimes of you and Gideon. You're just so close."

"You and me, we're close, too," he says, and I can tell how much he means it. "Gideon's a different kind of close. There's no way to compare you guys."

"I guess I just hoped that you liked me enough from the start to tell me this stuff."

"I did like you from the start. And it's not a measurement of my feelings for you. It's mostly just about when I felt comfortable enough to share. I wasn't walking around feeling guilty about you not knowing. It wasn't taking anything away from us. I wanted to make sure we'd be together for a while before I told you. I don't know why. I guess I wanted to make sure you liked me enough first."

I make an exaggerated frowny face at him. "That is so cute."

"Thanks," he says.

"Wanna go back to the dance? There should be one more slow song."

"Yeah, I definitely have time for one more slow song."

We link hands and walk back to the gym, just in time for one last slow song.

four

Gideon

I've been home from the dance for a couple of hours and I can't sleep.

Kyle texted me a while ago to say that he and Ruby made up and everything is fine between them. He said he'd tell me all about it in the morning. But I don't think I want to hear about it in the morning.

I can't stop running this whole situation over in my mind. Maybe I shouldn't have told Kyle to apologize to Ruby. Maybe I should have listened more before giving him advice. Maybe I should have told Buster to shut up. Maybe that was my big moment to tell Kyle how I feel about him.

But you can't tell someone how you feel when you don't

really know yourself. I couldn't make some big sweeping declaration of love when I feel so unsettled about everything.

It's after midnight. My parents are in bed. I've been lying here in my room since I got home, hoping that maybe if I just concentrate hard enough, I'll be able to figure out how I feel about Kyle. Or at least go to sleep. It's not working.

I trudge downstairs to watch TV. I could watch in my room, but I think if I spend one more second in my bed I might actually lose my mind.

I put on *Parks and Recreation* in hopes that it will lull me to sleep. But then Leslie Knope is going on about time management and binders and getting things done, and I know what I need to do.

It's time to get organized.

I tiptoe back upstairs and go into the back of my closet, where I have a shelf full of three-ring binders of various sizes. I select a navy-blue one-inch binder, because that seems like it should be big enough. Then I grab a ream of loose-leaf paper from my desk along with a ruler and my lucky pen. Because crooked lines are never an option.

Down in the den, I spread all my supplies out on the coffee table and turn off the TV. It's time to concentrate.

My first list is obviously a to-do list.

- Research: Am I gay or just into Kyle?
- Figure out what I'm going to do about being into Kyle. Because whether I'm gay or not, I'm pretty obviously into Kyle.

- Organize feelings.

- Create a plan of action.

I realize quickly there's not much more I can do at the moment, but I already feel more in control.

I flip to the next page and start a T chart with the heading "Am I gay or Kyle-sexual?" On one side I write reasons I think I'm gay, and on the other I write reasons I think this is just about Kyle. The number one reason I think it's just about Kyle is because I've literally never liked anyone else before. In my entire life. I can't remember being attracted to anyone.

I go through celebrities, models, athletes. I can understand how someone might find these people aesthetically pleasing, but I don't think I've ever imagined kissing anyone until I imagined kissing Kyle in the locker room.

But using the transitive property—if a = b and b = c, then a = c—I figure I'm both gay and in love with Kyle. Because Kyle is male and so am I. Simple as that.

I take a moment to adjust to this idea.

I am gay. I, Gideon Isaac Berko, am gay. It actually makes a lot of sense.

The next blank page becomes a list of reasons Kyle and I will never work out. The crux of the issue, aside from him having a girlfriend, is that I am not anything like Chris Evans, since apparently that's the type of guy Kyle likes.

I am the antithesis of Chris Evans. I could be in a remake of the Arnold Schwarzenegger and Danny DeVito classic *Twins*. Chris Evans would be the Arnold character and I, of course, would be there in all my DeVito-esque glory to play opposite him. I scribble all of this down, just trying to keep my thoughts in order, no matter how embarrassing they might be.

The grandfather clock in the living room chimes twice, alerting me to the fact that it's already two in the morning. I've been working on these lists for almost two hours.

I shake my head to clear it and flip to another clean sheet of paper, starting another list, this one about all the ways I like Kyle. Because damn, I really like Kyle, and I need to get them down on paper. I start with shallow stuff but soon find that I get more and more detailed.

I have a feeling this list might get embarrassing, so I decide to write it in Elvish.

Reasons to Like Kyle:

1. He's tall and can reach things on the top shelf.
2. He's adorably awkward and endearing and easy to like. Everyone likes him, not just me.
3. He's not one of those guys who never shuts up about his car.
4. He's not a jealous person.
5. Our shared love of Lord of the Rings makes us better friends.
6. Even though he has a girlfriend, he still has time to be friends with me. I was really worried when they first got together that I'd never see him anymore. But he's really loyal.
7. He listens to me babble about wanting to be

student council president even though he doesn't really care about that stuff.

8. We have varied interests but still get along really well.
9. He's always willing to help me with SAT vocab prep.
10. He tries new things even when he doesn't think he's going to like them.

I read over what I wrote, and it's embarrassing. Oh man, so embarrassing. I actually start blushing, by myself, in the middle of my own den just thinking about how much I like him. It's so ridiculous to put him on this high a pedestal, because if anyone is aware of how not-perfect Kyle is, that person is me. I've seen him at his best, but I've also seen him at his worst.

I have—I hate myself even as I think the word—a *crush*. I have a crush on my best friend. I have become a teen rom-com cliché. There is no hope for me.

I'm in desperate need of a dose of reality.

I flip one more page and start my last list by going through each of the reasons I like him and trying to think of a corresponding reason I don't.

Everything That's Wrong with Kyle:
1. He's too tall.
2. He's really awkward sometimes.
3. He's a terrible driver.
4. He's not as smart as me.

5. When I gave him the Lord of the Rings trilogy to read, he said he just "couldn't get into it." I even tried to get him to read _The Hobbit_ and he wouldn't. And that's practically a kids' book.
6. He has a girlfriend.
7. He doesn't care about school politics.
8. He's too into video games.
9. He has a limited vocabulary, and I always have to explain words to him.
10. He didn't get _Inception_. Or _The Matrix_. Or _Looper_. Or any of those awesome movies that are a little confusing.

About halfway through, I realized that I should probably be writing this one in Elvish, too, but it's getting late and I'm having focusing issues. I promise myself that I'm not going to keep this list. It's pretty brutal, but when you've been best friends with someone for twelve years, you know all the good and bad things about them.

But I finish it because it kind of feels good, cleansing, to get some of these things down on paper. I'm about to rip it up and throw it away, but then I'm startled by a noise at the front door. Someone's banging around, obviously trying to get inside.

Perhaps it's a really inept burglar?

I glance around the room, looking for something to use as a weapon, when I hear a familiar voice in the foyer.

"Ah, shit, crap," the person says as something falls over.

I walk into the hall and find my brother, Ezra, standing there.

The prodigal son returns in all his tattooed glory.

Ezra

I knock over a lamp on the side table next to the door. That seems like a good way to announce my return home in the middle of the night. It's sure to put everyone in the family in a great mood. I haven't been home since last Thanksgiving, so hopefully they'll be happy to see me anyway.

"I didn't know you were coming home," someone says in a gruff voice.

I look up, and there stands Gideon in a pair of very matchy-matchy pajamas with anchors all over them. Definitely a gift from our mother.

"It's great to see you, Giddyup." I juggle my rolling suitcase through the door, nearly knocking over the antique umbrella stand that no one has ever put an umbrella in.

He rolls his eyes. "No, but really, did Mom and Dad fail to tell me you were coming home or am I having a mini stroke?"

"I'm home for Passover," I say.

"You're a few days early."

"It's never too early to celebrate," I say with a smile.

He still looks perturbed, but then he sighs and pads over to me in his bare feet to give me a hug. A very tight hug. The kind of hug that makes me feel happy to be home.

He pulls away without a word and walks back toward the den. I follow him and find the coffee table a mess of paper and office supplies.

"You're really burning the midnight oil, huh?"

"It's a, um," Gideon stumbles and stammers as he collects all his papers and shoves them into a binder. It's probably killing him not to organize them in a neat and orderly fashion, but it's pretty obvious that he doesn't want me to read whatever's written on them.

"I'm just working on something for my, um, election campaign."

"So you've still got your eye on the big prize?" I ask, trying to get him to be more Gideon-like, because whoever this person is fluttering around the coffee table like a demonic bird is not my little brother. I obviously caught him doing something that he didn't expect to be caught doing. Some kind of strange, middle-of-the-night, illicit paperwork. Maybe a scandal is rocking the world of high school politics.

I slump into our father's Barcalounger, the one no one else is allowed to sit in if he's around, and try not to be too nosy. It was hard to miss the fact that some of the papers were written in Elvish. He slides everything under the couch and then sits primly down on it as if he's afraid he might crush his paperwork.

"So, how long are you planning to be in town?" he asks. His demeanor is making me even more curious about what he's trying to hide.

"What are you, interviewing me for the school paper?"

"Shut up," he says, finally smiling after what seems like forever. He's like a piñata of tension. I'm about to comment on it when there's a shriek in the hallway.

"Ezra!"

"Hi, Ma," I say, standing up to give her a hug and let her kiss me way too many times. My mom is a kisser. She kisses everyone. She'll kiss anyone if they stand still long enough. And if they don't, she'll chase them down.

"Maurice," she screams in between laying kisses on my forehead. "Maurice! Ezra's home!"

My father runs down the stairs in boxer shorts and a deep-cut V-neck undershirt, as usual. It's the image of childhood breakfasts. He adjusts his glasses at the bottom of the stairs.

"Ezra," he says with a grin. "It's good to see you."

He pulls me away from my mom and gives me a hug that lasts a long time, with plenty of pats on the back. He smells the same, like peppermint and aftershave. He used to always smell like tobacco, too, but my mom finally made him stop smoking a pipe.

"We had no idea you were coming," she says, straightening my hoodie like it's school picture day. "Why didn't you tell us? I would have had something prepared."

"It's fine, Ma," I say. "I really don't need anything. I was just talking to Gideon."

Our parents finally notice Gideon sitting on the couch, pouting like he's about three years old and not getting enough attention at a family gathering.

"I thought you went to bed hours ago," Mom says.

"I did. But you forgot to tie me down," he mutters, crossing his arms.

I laugh. I can't help it.

My father tsks but smiles, and my mother ignores Gideon.

Kid's got sass and sarcasm down pat. It's really the only

way to make it through being a teenager in this house. I totally understand.

And then my dad asks the question I've been worried to answer.

"So what are you doing here, pal?"

"Just wanted to see you guys," I say.

I don't tell them that I ran out of money. I don't tell them that I'm here indefinitely. For now I'll let them shower me with food and praise and let them act like it's not two o'clock in the morning.

But I'll have to tell them soon enough.

five

Kyle

I spend a lot of time during the next week trying to be invisible. This isn't really a recent development. I've always been more comfortable with being out of the spotlight. But between all this attention from the team winning state and my problems with English and my fight with Ruby, I need some "me time." This has been made much easier by the fact that it's Passover so Gideon has all these seders to go to with his family, leaving my evenings wide open to hide under my bed. Not just under the covers, but literally under my bed. I need that much coverage.

The biggest activity I really focus on is avoiding Ms. Gupta. No matter how much effort I put into pretending I'm not in class, she always seems to call on me. I need to work harder on not existing.

I figured that after I spent the whole weekend and most of this week working on her extra-credit assignment, maybe she'd go easy on me. I was wrong. I am always wrong.

Yesterday she wanted me to answer a question about how two random books we read this year were connected. I barely remember either of them. How can I possibly know what themes connect them? If she's so smart, she should already know how they're connected and not have to ask people about it.

What really sucks about the whole situation in her class is that I want to answer. Like, it would be awesome to be one of those kids, one of those people, who just understand things and answer questions like it's nothing. I don't think I ever noticed before how much I don't *get*. But, like, I do fine in all my classes. Unless maybe I'm not doing fine in all my classes and my teachers can't stand me so they keep passing me along.

That doesn't seem possible.

Obviously, they might not like me, that's completely possible, but the idea that they would pass a student just to get rid of them seems unlikely. It would seem to go against everything they believe as teachers.

Of course Ms. Gupta pulls me aside as I'm leaving class on Friday afternoon. But now that basketball is over, I have no excuse to make a fast getaway, even if Ruby is meeting me at my locker. Meeting your girlfriend to hang out isn't considered reason enough not to talk to your teacher, I would assume.

But this afternoon was special because Ruby finally doesn't have to babysit for once. She's always had a lot of responsibility at home, but lately it seems like there's more and more. I don't want to miss even a couple of minutes of hanging out with her, but I guess I have no choice.

"I finished going over your extra credit," Ms. Gupta says.

I make a noise somewhere between a yawn and a groan. Invisible people should not make noise. *Pretend to be a tree, pretend to be a tree*, I tell myself. *Trees don't speak.*

"It's not great, Kyle. I'm a little concerned that you rushed through it."

She seems to be waiting for me not to be a tree, but all I can manage to do is chew on my bottom lip.

"It's enough to push you into D range for the marking period, but that's not exactly a victory. I think you need to consider getting a tutor."

"Oh."

"If you could pull your grade up to a B next marking period, this blip won't seem so bad in the grand scheme of things. I'm still a little worried that there's something else going on, but you don't have to tell me about it."

"There's nothing else going on," I say, my voice sounding thin and nervous to my own ears, and I hate the guy I become when I'm put on the spot like this. I clear my throat. "I mean, I'm not having some kind of crisis at home or whatever you might be thinking."

She smiles a thin-lipped smile. "Well, I guess you should get out of here then, but before you go, here's a list of available peer tutors."

I take a quick look at it, and of course Gideon is right at the top.

"Do you know anyone on that list who you don't mind asking for help? If not, I can get someone assigned to you."

"No, I know someone."

We say good-bye, and I shove the list into the bottom of my backpack.

This sucks, this sucks, this sucks, I think as I walk to my locker.

"Hey there, Mr. Crabby Pants."

I'm so annoyed and lost in thought that I didn't even notice I was getting closer to my locker, and I definitely didn't notice Ruby standing in front of it.

"Oh, hi," I say, kissing her cheek. At least things with Ruby and me are better.

"What's up?" she asks, looking concerned. "I don't think I've ever seen you looking that pissed-off before. It's a weird look for you."

I try to pull in all the air I can and rearrange my face into a more relaxed expression. I can *feel* how tense I am. I can only imagine how tense I must look.

"Um. I didn't do very well on an English assignment. No big deal." It's not a complete lie.

"Is that really all?" she asks, examining me from several angles as I kneel down in front of my locker and try to figure out what I need to take home with me tonight. I always keep a list going on a notepad of what's due the next day, but I can't find my notepad at the moment and everything feels wrong.

"Yeah, it's nothing. Not a big deal. I just needed to talk to Ms. Gupta."

"She's so awesome."

Hearing Ruby declare my greatest enemy "awesome" is too much to take. I don't even care what's due on Monday. I'll care later when my mom asks me about what homework I need to do this weekend, and I'll care next week when I don't have anything to turn in, but right now, I do not care.

I shove whatever's closest in my bag and stand up, slamming my locker door closed.

"Guess you're not a fan?"

"Oh, uh . . ." I shake my head. "I mean she did just give me a bad grade, but I'll get over it." I smile. It's forced, but it seems to make Ruby feel better. I take her hand and pull her in for a real kiss.

She smiles into it and then backs away. "That's more like it," she says.

I take a deep breath and feel a lot calmer. I lean on the lockers and realize that my notepad was in my back pocket the whole time.

"You ready to get out of here?" she asks.

"In one second. I think I forgot something."

I kneel back down, open my locker, and take a minute to read my notes and make sure I have everything organized. I'll show Ms. Gupta that I'm just fine and that I have everything under control. I'll ask Gideon to tutor me, maybe leaving out the part where I'm failing and focusing on the part where I just want to keep my grades up for basketball camp. I know it doesn't make any sense to try to hide this grade when my parents will find out on my report card in a couple of weeks, but maybe they'll be less angry if they know that I'm already being proactive about my grades.

I finally have the right books in my bag for the weekend and I'm ready to go. This time I close my locker with a smaller slam. It's weird how much better I feel than even just a couple of minutes ago.

As we're about to leave, Gideon strolls up.

Gideon

"What's up, Gid?" Kyle asks when he sees me.

"You're giving me a ride home? And we're supposed to hang out tonight? We made plans, like, three days ago." I knew he'd forget. He always forgets this stuff.

"Oh crap!" he says, smacking his forehead.

"I knew you'd forget," I say.

"It's just that Ruby doesn't have to babysit for once," he starts explaining really fast. "And I had to stay after to talk to Gupta again, and I didn't forget. I just kind of didn't think about it."

I nod. "It happens," I say.

"But it's your birthday weekend," Kyle says. "We were supposed to start our marathon."

"It's cool, don't worry about it," I say.

At the same time, Ruby says, "I could go home. I don't mind."

"Maybe the three of us could do something together?" Kyle asks, glancing between Ruby and me. "You guys can come back to my house and we can hang out?"

Every single bone in my body says no. I can't imagine a worse situation at the moment than having to hang out with them being all lovey-dovey and couple-y. Not that they're really one of those couples, but almost anything could be too much in my current fragile state of liking Kyle.

I look over at Ruby, hoping that she's not into the idea, but she's smiling and nodding. This is terrible.

We hop into Kyle's car, and I tell myself it's not going to be so bad. That I have this all under control. Even though I have a feeling it's going to be pretty awkward when it's all said and done.

As soon as we walk into Kyle's house, it's apparent that we're not going to be able to hang out there.

His sisters have every single member of the middle school softball team over for a start-of-the-season pizza party. The sheer volume of squealing will not be conducive to anything that requires concentration.

"What should we do?" Kyle asks.

"It's cool," I say. "We can go hang out at my house."

But when we walk in my front door, the peace and quiet is almost deafening, and I have no idea how I'm supposed to entertain Ruby. I know how to entertain Kyle. I've had years of practice, but I have no clue what Ruby's into. I should know more about her, since she's been my best friend's girlfriend for six months. But all I know is that she loves cheerleading and she spends a lot of time with her family.

"So what do you guys want to do?" I ask.

Kyle chews on his lip. "Um, maybe we should have grabbed my PS4 while we were at my house. Ruby's a big fan of Grand Theft Auto."

"Are you really?" I ask.

"Yeah, it's not so bad," she says.

Kyle gives me a meaningful look. "Would you mind helping

♥ 55 ♥

me get all the stuff together for it?" he asks. "You know I never grab the right cables or whatever."

"Um, sure," I say.

"Ruby, you stay here," he says quickly. "Go hang out in the den and we'll be right back."

Ruby looks a little taken aback, but she seems to follow his directions as we head out the front door and back to Kyle's house.

As soon as we're alone in Kyle's room, he starts talking. "I need your help, but I don't really want to tell anyone else, but I know I can trust you."

"Of course, anything."

"I'm doing kind of bad in English, and I need you to tutor me," he says. He licks his lips. "Please."

"Oh," I say. "Um, sure, of course."

"Gupta gave me your name on a list of peer tutors, so I figured you'd be into it."

"Definitely." I scratch my head. "What do you need to do?"

He shrugs. "Nothing right now. I have a paper due in a couple of weeks, but I turned in an extra-credit essay and that didn't go well. So she told me about the peer tutoring thing."

"How bad are you doing?"

He scrunches up his nose. Oh God, he's too cute.

"Well, I'm getting a D this marking period."

"Ouch."

"Yeah, and I need to keep my GPA above a C so I don't lose my spot at that basketball camp this summer."

"We'll figure it out," I say. "I promise."

He grins and seems more himself already.

six

Ruby

I've always been aware of the fact that Kyle and Gideon live next door to each other. Their houses are definitely similar to look at them from the outside, like you can tell that someone tried to build them in the same style. Gideon's house is obviously a little bigger and a little older. But I expected it to be a normal-person house.

I did not expect it to be a freaking mansion on the inside.

When Kyle and Gideon leave me alone, I can't help but wander around a little.

His house has this gigantic foyer with big stairs and a couple of doorways off it. I'm sure they just think of it as a hall-way or something. Really rich people are always downplaying how rich they are.

I take a peek into each door as I pass and find the exact kind of super ridiculously fancy parlor you would expect on one side, with an equally fancy dining room on the other. Then there's a family room with a big-ass TV, and finally the kitchen. But even the kitchen is bigger than I would expect, with an island and a separate eat-in area, like a breakfast nook. There's one room beyond the kitchen, like a big sun porch. Maybe it's called a solarium. I don't know, my *House Hunters* addiction has only gotten me so far in life, and my parents recently canceled our cable anyway.

His mom is in the kitchen, looking really put together and a little too smiley for my taste.

"Hi," I say. "I'm Ruby, Kyle's girlfriend."

"Hi," she says, extending her hand to shake mine. "I'm Miriam Berko."

I never quite know how to respond to adults who tell me their first name like that. Am I supposed to say, "A real pleasure to meet you, Miriam. You have a lovely home"?

Mrs. Berko shakes my hand up and down like it's one of those old-fashioned water pumps and offers me a snack.

"No thanks, I'm good," I tell her, my smile plastered on. I'm honestly a little bit worried my face might get stuck like this.

"Gideon and Kyle went back over to Kyle's to get his PS4," I tell her. "So I'm just going to wait for them in the den. If that's okay."

"Sure, of course," she says.

I make my way back into the den and sit in the chair that looks the most used. And even then it doesn't look like anyone ever really sits in it, but more like they bought it that way.

I try to find a comfortable position, but in the process my phone slides out of my pocket and under the couch.

When I reach to grab it, at first I pull out a binder that's super disheveled and has paper coming out the edges. I swear I don't mean to peek, but the edge of one has some writing on it and I can't miss Kyle's name. My natural nosiness takes over and I slide it out.

It's a to-do list. A to-do list about Gideon liking Kyle. And not in a friend way, like in a pretty obviously romantic way. There are tons of lists, each one more damning than the last. One of them is in Elvish, and something tells me that's probably the worst of them all.

I stop for a second and take in what I'm looking at.

Not only is Gideon gay, but he's in love with my boyfriend. Or at least in some pretty deep like with my boyfriend. It's a lot to take in, and who knows when someone might walk into this room. I snap a picture of each list with my phone, because I want to understand better what's going on. And because I'm just plain nosy. I really can't help it.

As I slide the binder back under the couch, the front door opens and closes and footsteps trail down the hall before they pause at the door.

"Hi," a male voice says. A male voice attached to a complete hottie who is neither Gideon nor Kyle.

EZRA

"Hey yourself," she says.

"Ruby, right?" I ask. She was a freshman when I was a senior. Even back then everyone knew who Ruby Vasquez was.

"Yeah," she says, nodding coolly and turning to look at me. "Ezra, right?"

"Yeah. I wasn't sure you'd remember."

"Hell yeah, I remember," she says, breaking out into a grin. "You're basically a legend at Madison High. Getting out of this stupid town and heading to L.A. to become a surfer is still one of the coolest things anyone from here has ever done."

I grin. I can't help myself. That was pretty cool of me. Until my bar mitzvah money ran out. And then my graduation money. And then I realized that working at Starbucks thirty hours a week wasn't going to cut it.

But she doesn't need to know about that stuff.

"I heard you were doing really well, too. Like winning some kind of tournament."

I have no idea who would have started such a rumor, but I thank them in my head.

"Oh totally. I'm just home for Passover."

"Isn't that almost over? Are you leaving soon?"

"Um. Not sure." I did not expect this chick to know when Passover was, so instead I go for a quick change of subject. I survey the room, trying to think of something else to talk about.

"I can only imagine how desperate you are to get back to California," she continues.

"Totally. So what are you doing here?" I ask, deciding to go with the obvious.

"Well, we were supposed to be playing Grand Theft Auto,

but Kyle and Gideon went over to his house to get the PS4 and have abandoned me here."

"Do you want something to drink?" I ask, gesturing toward the kitchen.

"Nah, I'm good," she says. "What's California like? Is it everything you wanted it to be?"

"Um, it was good. I had a lot of fun. Met a lot of people." I realize too late that I'm talking in the past tense, but if Ruby notices, she doesn't say anything.

"Well, it looks like it suits you," she says, giving me an appraising look just as Kyle and Gideon come in through the back door.

"I'm so sorry about making you wait, Ruby," Gideon says. "And about him." He points in my direction.

"What about me?" I ask. "I was just being cordial to your guest."

"It's really no big deal," she says. Kyle sits down on the sofa next to her and puts his arm around her shoulders.

"Sorry that took so long," he says to her. Then he turns to me like he just noticed I was here. "How's it going, Ezra? Gideon told me you were back, but I haven't seen you around much."

"Yeah, I've been hiding in my cave," I say seriously.

"Well, it's good to see you," he says.

I have to wonder if he could sense there was a little vibe going on between Ruby and me while we were waiting for them. Personally, I can't help but notice there's something going on between Gideon and Kyle. Like they were just telling secrets.

They're never this quiet around each other. Unless it's for Ruby's benefit. That's gotta be a weird dynamic. It's never fun to be the third wheel.

I consider for a moment hanging out with them, but Gideon's hooking up the PS4 and Ruby and Kyle are talking. They don't need me. I head up to my room for another round of reruns on cable instead.

seven

Gideon

After way too many hours spent playing video games, Kyle and Ruby leave and I clean up the family room. My parents went out for dinner a little while ago and Ezra is still upstairs in his cave, and it's kind of nice to be alone to think.

About halfway through the afternoon I started thinking about how guilty I feel about my list of things that are wrong with Kyle. I stop cleaning and realize that the binder I wrote the list in has been sitting under the couch for the past week.

I fish it out and flip the pages to the terrible, horrible, really mean list.

I read it over again and my stomach turns. Now that I know he's having trouble in school, some of the stuff on here feels even more harsh and personal. Like I'm mocking his hard time. There's only one solution.

Kill it with fire.

I grab the grill lighter from the junk drawer in the kitchen and go out to the back deck. I'm looking around for a metal bucket that my mom keeps out here for gardening when Ezra comes out behind me.

"Why did you leave the door open? It's freaking freezing out here!" he says, rubbing his arms.

"You have thin California blood now. It's fifty-seven degrees outside, which is really pretty nice for New Jersey in April."

"Shut up," he says. He notices the lighter and the piece of paper. "What are you doing?"

"Nothing," I say, even though it's obviously a lie.

"Sure, sure," he says, about to reach for the list.

"Don't touch that."

He holds his hands up in surrender. "So, what's the deal with Ruby?"

"What do you mean?" I ask.

"Are you into her?" he asks.

"She's dating Kyle."

"Doesn't mean you can't be into her," he says as he folds his arms and leans against the doorjamb.

"The fact that I'm gay does," I mutter. It's out in the air before I'm even fully aware of what I'm saying. I slap a hand over my mouth instinctively and look up at Ezra, whose jaw is basically on the floor.

"Jesus Christ," Ezra says.

"He doesn't have anything to do with this," I say, trying my best to regain my composure. I rub my hands over my face and turn to give him my full attention. "I actually only recently realized it."

"That's a pretty big deal, Giddyup."

"It's not really."

"Did you tell Mom and Dad yet?"

"No."

"Can I be there when you do? Because let's be real, they're going to be so excited. Mom especially. I'm sure she has a list of guys she could set you up with."

I can't help but grin because he's so right. "So you should know that you're kind of the first person I've told."

"Seriously? Me?"

"Yes. Why would I lie about that?" I ask, finally finding the bucket under the deck steps.

"Fair point," he says.

I crush the offensive list in a ball and toss it in the bucket. Then I lean over and set that sucker on fire with the long-handled lighter.

"So is this some kind of ritual burning?" Ezra asks. "Some kind of hazing to get you into the gay guy club?"

I look at him and then back at the little fire that's already burning itself out. I think about telling him about Kyle, about the list, about everything I'm dealing with. I'm not there yet. Maybe when I am, Ezra would be a good person to talk to. But for now, I go along with his jokes.

"Yes. I am now a full-fledged member of what is technically the Order of Men Who Love Other Men."

"Ah yes, OMWLOM. Very prestigious."

I dump out the ash that's in the bucket, and then Ezra and I head back inside, where he forces me to watch a marathon of classic eighties TV shows.

But not before I hide the binder safely away in the Monopoly box under my bed.

Ruby

The second I get home, I know something is wrong. My parents sit at our kitchen table, their faces gray with worry.

"We'll talk in the morning," my mom says, shooing me in the direction of the bedroom I share with my little sister. My brothers, David and Marco, share one, and Diana and I share the other. My parents sleep on a pullout couch in the living room. They say it's not so bad, but I know they're lying.

I sit down across from them.

"Can we please talk now?" I say. "This just doesn't seem to be the time to start treating me like a little kid."

My dad shows me a memo from his job. They're cutting third shift. His shift.

"What does this mean? Can you get a different job? Move to a different time or something?" I ask, knowing even as I say the words that they wouldn't look so worried if that was a possibility.

My dad shakes his head.

I chew my lip and look around my house. It's nothing like Gideon's, that's for damn sure.

"I know what you're thinking," my mom says. "And don't you worry about it. We have it all under control."

"I could get a job," I offer.

"No," my dad says quickly.

"Why not? I'm eighteen. I should be working anyway."

"You need to concentrate on school," my mom says, the old refrain. No matter how hard things get, they're always so much more worried about me getting good grades than how much I could be helping with money.

"But—"

My dad cuts me off. "We're going to need more help watching the kids. Mom's going to get a second job, and I'm going to take whatever I can as soon as I can."

I swallow hard.

"And we'll cut wherever we can," he adds.

There's not much more to cut, I think but don't say out loud. Things have been lean around here for a while, which makes me wonder how long he's known this might be a possibility.

After a few more minutes, I go to bed. But I don't sleep.

eight

Gideon

I make my way up the front walk at Kyle's house, and he must have been watching for me. He yanks open his front door and without a word, I shove my license into his hands.

"Awesome," he says. "Now you can drive sometimes."

"I can drive sometimes if and when my parents ever get me a car."

"Is there an estimate for that?"

"When my mom finally picks out a new car, I get her current one. But she claims that I can borrow it whenever, since she works from home."

Kyle nods appreciatively and we walk into the kitchen, where we collect every potential snack food and head down into the basement.

"You ready for this?" he asks.

"I was born ready."

"Oh yeah, happy birthday, or whatever."

"Thanks or whatever," I say.

We settle in to watch the first movie. We tend not to talk too much during the first few hours of it. It's become almost a spiritual thing between us.

"There's nothing wrong with this movie," Kyle says, restarting a conversation that we've had a million times, to the point where we each have our own set of lines and cues as we discuss it.

"Absolutely not. It's basically a masterpiece."

"It's just, some of the acting . . ."

"It's so over the top," I say, finishing his sentence as I always do.

At that moment on-screen Frodo is kicking Boromir's ass.

"I can't handle it when he looks up and pushes his hair back from his face," Kyle says, giggling.

"Frodo," I say, in a near-perfect imitation of Boromir. I honestly couldn't tell you if anyone else on earth finds this as funny as we do, but in the grand scheme of things, that doesn't matter. What matters is that we find it hilarious.

By the time we finish the first one, we've eaten all the snacks we brought down and decide to order a pizza.

"So where are your parents?" I ask while we wait for it to arrive. It seemed sort of dumb to get into *The Two Towers* if we were just going to get interrupted by the doorbell twenty minutes in.

"They took my sisters into the city to see some show."

"Well that was super nice of them," I say as the doorbell rings, signaling the arrival of our pizza.

"I love these extended editions. I don't know why they didn't just do the extended editions in the movies," I say.

"I love that you talk about this so authoritatively, as if you weren't three when the movies were in the theaters."

"I can have opinions about anything I want to have opinions about," I reply.

"My opinion is that Elijah Wood is supercute." This is the first time Kyle has ever mentioned being attracted to someone who even remotely looks like me. And I'm not saying I look like Elijah Wood, but I am short and dark-haired. It's just nice to hear about someone besides Chris Evans.

We make it through the second movie, agreeing as usual that Gimli is the best part and the Tree Ents are weird but cool. Kyle runs upstairs to warm up the pizza and when he comes back down, he sits a little closer to me on the sofa.

When we finish our next slices and lean back on the couch, our shoulders are touching, and they stay that way for almost the entirety of the third movie. I can barely watch. I can only think about that little bit of contact.

At least until we get to the epilogues.

Kyle starts sniffling next to me, so I look over at him.

"I'm sorry!" he says, wiping his eyes and then crossing his arms. "I just really like how they weave all this together at the end. And it's really about friendship, you know?"

I hold his gaze for a beat too long and can't deny the fact that I kind of feel like kissing him.

He's just so Kyle-earnest and sensitive and kind.

I bite my bottom lip, but I don't look away. I have to close my eyes for a second, though, because it's all too much. I don't understand what's happening.

I open my eyes and his gaze is locked on mine, like he had taken the opportunity to observe me while my eyes were closed.

"Have I ever told you that I think you look like Elijah Wood?"

I laugh in surprise and glance away. "You have definitely never mentioned that."

We make eye contact again and he still looks a little sad, like his eyes are sort of wet, but he's also smiling. He surveys my face, and more than anything I want to know what he's thinking. I want to know what would happen if I leaned in and put my lips gently on his. Of course, my whole body chooses that moment to betray me and I actually do lean in a little.

He blushes. His jaw drops and his eyes trail away.

But I recover by making a big production of pulling my phone out of my pocket. There's a pretty good chance that was the slickest thing I've ever done. Because for a second there, it looked like I was trying to kiss him.

I take a look at my phone and have a text from Ruby.

Weird.

Ruby

Things have gone from bad to worse at my house during the past twenty-four hours. My parents told my sister and brothers about my dad losing his job. I don't know that they all really understand what's happening, but I think they can tell by our parents' expressions that it's hard times at the Vasquez house.

Not that we've ever been living in the lap of luxury, but this is above and beyond what we're used to. I didn't even bother asking about college yet, even though it's all I can think about. Something told me that it wasn't the right time to bring it up. I'm not going anywhere impressive, just to the rinky-dink state university about a half hour away. I have an academic scholarship at least. But up until now, I had every intention of living on campus. That probably won't happen anymore.

I pick up my phone, thinking I should call Kyle and tell him everything. That would make me feel so much better. Except even as I'm about to scroll to his number, I remember that he and Gideon are hanging out together.

And then I remember the lists.

The lists that I totally forgot about until right this second. Guess I'm not as nosy as I thought. I take a quick scroll through the pictures, and there are twelve lists in total.

Most of them don't seem very interesting. I scan for the to-do list I saw last time. There are only a few things on it, and a lot of them are crossed off.

Gideon is gay, and very in the closet.

And not only that, but he's in love with my boyfriend and his best friend.

I know too much. I should delete these lists and never think about them again.

Any other time in my life I might actually have been sympathetic to this issue and done exactly that. But jealousy starts bubbling up in my stomach. I'm always so nice to Gideon. I'm always encouraging Kyle to spend more time with him and to be a good friend and all that crap. And this is how Gideon repays me?

How long has he had feelings for Kyle?

Does Kyle know? Is that why he finally told me he's bi, because he's thinking about breaking up with me for Gideon? Is he preparing me for that inevitability?

Gideon has everything already. His parents are rich; he'll have no trouble getting into whatever college he wants, not to mention he won't have to worry about affording it. Now on top of that he wants my boyfriend, too? I can't handle it.

I'm suddenly so jealous of Gideon Berko it feels like I'm burning from the inside. My fingers are actually shaking with rage.

I do something I know I'll regret later. But I have to show him I know. I have to make sure he realizes how much power I have over him. He can't just go about his life, happily being in love with my boyfriend while living in a house that looks the way his house looks, with parents who have jobs and money.

I text him the picture of the list where he's trying to decide whether he's gay or just in love with Kyle. I follow it up with a text that simply says, "I know."

We'll see what he thinks of that.

Kyle

I swear about thirty seconds ago Gideon looked like he was about to kiss me, and now he looks like someone just punched him in the stomach.

"Are you okay?" I ask, pausing the movie. I don't want to miss the last couple of scenes.

He's pale and staring at his phone like it said something mean to him.

"Yeah, I'm fine," he says, gulping loudly.

"Did you get bad news?"

"Huh? No, nothing like that. Just . . ." He shoves his phone into his pocket but doesn't continue his sentence.

"Did I do something wrong?"

He finally looks over at me, and he has that same sweaty and confused look he had the night at the dance. I have to fight the urge to rub away the worry line that's on his forehead.

He shakes his head. "Definitely not. Let's just finish up the movie."

I swear before he checked his phone we were about to have a moment. There was something going on between us, and it's unsettling. It's the weirdest feeling. Because it makes me feel like I messed up somehow. But if I feel like I messed up, does that mean I wanted something to happen between us?

Gideon's my best friend. I really don't need to develop feelings for him. Not when I have a girlfriend. Not when he's straight.

At least, I think he's straight. He's never said anything about not being straight. And I have to assume that when I told him I was bi, he would have told me then if he was something other than straight.

He moves as far away from me on the couch as possible and then grabs for the remote, hitting PLAY before I can say anything else to him.

I cross my arms and try to understand what just happened. But maybe I don't even want to know.

As soon as the movie's over, Gideon's out the door in a

flash, and I'm left to clean up the mess we made in the basement.

I have this sinking feeling in my gut that I did something very wrong today. But I don't know what it is, and I don't know how to make it up to him.

There's this other thought, kind of creeping its way from the back of my brain as I pick up pieces of popcorn on the floor and make a pile of paper plates.

I think I might kind of like Gideon.

Like, *like* Gideon.

I shake the feeling away and tell myself to forget it.

nine

Gideon

A braver man would have texted Ruby back immediately with something cutting and witty to show her how much a text like that didn't bother him.

I am not that brave man.

Instead I spend most of Monday slinking around school and hiding as much as I can. I don't know how to deal with the issue, so I just don't. I avoid it, ignore it, and downright fall into denial about it.

The good news is that since I'm seventeen now, my mom's letting me borrow her car every day this week, so I can celebrate my newfound independence by driving myself to school.

That morning when I start up the car, I try not to imagine Kyle hopping over the fence in his very Kyle fashion and getting in the car with me. I very carefully do not imagine the conversation we'd be having, and I even more cautiously do not go anywhere near the thought of touching him.

There is no touching Kyle.

I do realize that I could allay a lot of my fears by asking Ruby what she's going to do. I honestly don't believe for a second she's the kind of person who would out me, but I could imagine her maybe holding this over my head somehow. Not in a blackmailing kind of way. But maybe that's only because I can't imagine what she would blackmail me for.

I'm slightly worried that Ruby's blackmailing me and I don't even know it.

The morning wears on in exhausting fashion. It's five minutes until lunch and I'm not quite sure what to do with myself. I've been eating at a lunch table with a mix of my friends and Kyle's friends lately, and I'm sure Ruby will be there. Waiting for me. Watching me like the weak little man I am.

The thought alone makes me sigh so loud during precalc that the kid sitting next to me takes a moment away from whatever it is we're supposed to be doing to glare at me like I let rip a silent but deadly fart rather than just a harmless exhale of lament. I glare right back. *Do not mess with me*, I tell him with my eyes. *I am having a serious shit storm of a day.*

Kyle finds me at my locker during passing time and corners me.

"Where have you been all day? You're like a Ringwraith slinking around school," he says, his eyes sparkling in a way that I hate myself for noticing.

"Just have a lot going on," I sputter out.

"I was a little surprised you left without me for school."

"Oh, um, I guess I figured we'd drive separately."

"You could have at least let me know before I waited for you," he says, his eyes a little less sparkly now and a little more hurt.

"I'm sorry," I say. "I guess I thought I mentioned it to you."

"You kind of ran off Saturday night," he says.

"Yeah, sorry," I say, trying to keep my attention on my locker so I don't have to stare into his eyes anymore.

"And we need to come up with some time to talk about tutoring," he says.

My stomach drops.

I'm supposed to be tutoring Kyle.

I am so conflicted.

Because on the one hand, it's not very professional of me to back out when I told him that I would help. I have my reputation as a peer tutor to uphold. On the other hand, there's a good chance that the girlfriend of the guy I'm supposed to be tutoring will kill me if I spend quality time with him.

I need to man up and talk to Ruby.

"So?" Kyle prods.

"Do you have something due soon?"

"I have that paper I told you about."

"All right, we'll figure it out," I promise.

But first I have to talk to your girlfriend.

I'm about to walk away, to eat my lunch alone in the student activity office and come up with a plan of action for talking to Ruby, but Kyle grabs my arm.

"And if you could maybe not tell anyone you're tutoring me?" he says, his voice crackling with nerves.

"Nobody knows you're having trouble?" I ask.

"Nobody but you, me, and Ms. Gupta."

"Oh."

Well, this just got a lot harder to deal with.

Ruby

I sneak up on Gideon because I know otherwise he might run away. But I need to talk to him. It's killing me not to talk to him about what I know.

I'm not gonna lie: the fact that he hasn't talked to me isn't helping his case. It makes me want to play with him, like a dog with a chew toy. It's not fair, but guess what? Life isn't fair. That's become very obvious to me lately.

Kyle told me that Gideon was heading in the direction of the student activity office last he saw him, so I make my way over there after I finish eating lunch.

When I get to the door of the office, I find Gideon sitting at the table in the center of the room, hunched over a sandwich and furiously writing in a composition notebook, like his whole life is a test.

"Knock, knock," I say, instead of actually knocking.

He gasps a little when he sees me, but he keeps his composure and sits up straight, folding his hands in his lap.

"Hello, Ruby."

"Hey." I take a seat across from him. "I thought you might come find me today, or you know, at least text me back."

"Um. Well." He licks his lips and takes a deep breath. "I wasn't really sure what you expected me to say."

"You're smart. I thought you'd figure something out."

He cracks his knuckles. "Fine. What do you want from me?"

"What makes you think I want something from you?"

"I don't know. Your semi-threatening text, your ominous appearance in what I like to think of as my safe space. I don't know what to make of the situation. You basically know all my secrets. I'd like to know what you're planning on doing with your knowledge." He swallows and stares at the table, like he's awaiting sentencing.

"It's just kind of funny, because recently I've noticed the way you look at Kyle."

"And how is that?"

"Like you want him. Like you want to steal him from me."

"The point of those lists wasn't that I wanted to 'steal' him from you," he says, making air quotes around the word.

"Then what was the point?"

"They were for me. I wanted to organize my thoughts and eventually find a way to get over him, since he's with you and he likes you. I don't want to come between you guys."

I'm not sure how to respond. It feels like he's telling the truth, but that would mean he has absolutely no idea of how much power he truly holds over Kyle. Is he really that oblivious?

"Are you actually threatened by me?" he asks.

"No, Gideon, I'm not threatened by you," I say, in the most bored voice I can muster.

"So you're not about to tell me to back off your man or something?"

"I'm not. He's your best friend. Wouldn't it look a little suspicious if you just suddenly stopped talking to him?"

"Yes, it would." He folds his arms and sits back in the chair. "I guess I'm just not sure what the point of this conversation is."

I probably should have had a better idea myself before I decided to challenge Gideon "King of the Forensics Team" Berko to a debate.

"I wanted to make sure we were on the same page."

"What page, Ruby?" he asks, obviously getting annoyed.

"You're going to make me spell it out to you?"

"Are you blackmailing me? I don't get it. So yeah, you're going to have to spell it out to me. Because the way I see it, you're backed into a corner. I'm pretty sure you have it in you to tell the whole school that I like Kyle, but you realize that in doing so you would also out me. And I'm pretty sure that you're too good a person for that. So I don't know where that leaves us."

I'm not sure what to say in response. I was going to make a few more thinly veiled threats about showing Kyle the lists, but he hit the nail on the head: I would never out him.

"So it's not like either of us has any power in the situation," he concludes as he stands up and collects his belongings.

"Let me know if you come up with some way to blackmail me," he says as he walks out the door.

I'm left sitting there with my jaw hanging open. I have no idea what I expected, but it was certainly not that.

Gideon

I'm shaking as I walk out of the office and leave Ruby in my wake.

When she walked in, I was working on the logic of the situation and realized that basically as long as I'm in the closet, I have all the power. Because there's no way she's going to out me. I believe that for a fact.

It's when I decide to come out that she could totally screw me. Those lists, particularly the one with all the mean things about Kyle, could really bite me in the ass. I would ask her to delete them, but I'm not sure how she would react.

But here's what I know for sure: I should probably avoid both of them for a little while. At least when they're together. And I should definitely avoid Ruby as much as humanly possible. It's the only option I see.

Of course, this is the week that Kyle decides to really turn on the charm. He's there every time I turn a corner; he's always saving the seat right next to him at lunch. I don't really know why he's doing it or what changed, but it makes me feel conspicuous. Like he and Ruby are concocting a plan together.

But no, Kyle would never do that.

The worst is on Tuesday, when he leaves a note in Elvish in my locker asking me when we can get together about tutoring. It's like a stab in the heart. I promise myself that I'll talk to him about it the next day.

By Friday at the latest.

Maybe I could go to his house this weekend when I'm certain Ruby's not around.

I wish I could understand when our friendship got so complicated.

ten

Kyle

On Wednesday when Ruby finds me after school, I can tell she's in a panic.

"I really need a huge favor from you," she says.

"What's up?" I ask, putting my books in my locker.

"My mom was supposed to pick up Diana from dance class, and I was supposed to go watch David move up a belt at karate. But now she can't make it and they won't let the kids leave with just anyone after dance class. So would you maybe be willing to go watch David get his new belt while I run across town in the other direction to pick up Diana?" She says all this so fast that it actually takes me a good ten seconds to catch up with everything.

"Yes. I can totally do that."

"Thank you so, so much," she says, kissing me on the cheek. Then she tells me the karate ceremony is at the rec center and I need to get there by four. She trots off after that, and I stand there for a second watching her go.

When I turn around, Gideon's at his locker down at the other end of the hall, filling up his bag. Maybe if I catch him by surprise, he'll have no choice but to talk to me. It's been a weird week between us, and it's only half over.

"Hey, so I know we haven't hung out at all lately and I don't know if it's something I did or what, but do you want to go with me to watch Ruby's brother's karate ceremony thing? Like, where he gets a new belt?" I say this all in such a rush that I can't help but trip over my words and lose track of exactly what I want to say. But I hope Gideon understands.

He stands up. "Why are you going?"

"Well, Ruby was supposed to go and now she can't, so she asked me to."

"So she won't be there?" he asks, not looking me in the eye.

"Nope."

He squares his shoulders and meets my eye. "Yeah, sure. It's not like I have anything else I was going to do."

"Cool."

"Who knows? Maybe it'll even be fun."

"Yeah. We could take him out for a slice of pizza after," I say, turning in the direction of the nearest exit.

"We could," Gideon agrees.

The drive over to the community center isn't far, but there are tons of stoplights and crossing guards on the way, making it really slow going.

"So where's Ruby?"

"She had to go pick up her sister, Diana, from dance class for her mom."

"It's really nice of her, to spend so much time with her brothers and sister."

I want to ask what's wrong with him, but I don't know how to force the topic. I chew my thumbnail and try to think of non-awkward ways to bring up the weird moment on his birthday. But what if I bring it up and that was never the issue to begin with? Or what if I bring it up and he realizes that I think we had a moment but we really didn't and it would basically be the most embarrassing thing that's ever happened to me?

I do not like Gideon, I tell myself.

"You look really perturbed," he says as we pull into the community center, my car quickly getting swallowed up in the sea of minivans and SUVs.

"What's perturbed mean?" I ask. Gideon never minds when I don't know his SAT vocabulary words. We both took the test back at the beginning of March. I'm definitely going to have to retake it, because I didn't do very well. Gideon did really, really well, but he's still planning to retake it next month. And he's still studying. He's really into the SAT.

"Like bothered, upset."

"Nah. I'm really glad you're here with me. It makes me feel less weird about being here. This is a lot of moms."

"It really is," he agrees as we make our way to the community center meeting room. It is packed wall-to-wall with moms, and dads, and grandmas. And what seems like maybe every crying toddler in town.

"Last chance to run away," I say as we find seats in the back row.

"Heck no, I'm in it for the long haul. And moms love me. It's you they're always kind of iffy about."

"No way! Moms love me way more than they love you," I say, shouting to be heard over the din at the same moment it gets quiet.

Three moms look over at us and give us a dirty look for causing a ruckus.

"I love that they gave us a dirty look when that three-year-old is being louder than everyone else in this room put together," Gideon whispers as a guy in a karate uniform comes up to the microphone and introduces himself as the sensei at the community center.

"I could be that loud," I say, trying to start a staring contest with the three-year-old. He stares right back, and I'm quite frankly ever so slightly intimidated.

"I honestly don't think you could."

"You're right."

I knock our knees together and hope Gideon understands how much I've missed him lately.

Gideon

Okay, so I'll admit it. Life is better with your best friend, even if you're in love with him and sometimes have to deal with weird non-threats from his girlfriend.

I can't deny that as soon as Kyle told me what was happening with Ruby, I saw the afternoon for the opportunity that it was.

If she was off helping her sister, I would have several hours of pure, unadulterated Kyle time. We still had to hang out with Ruby's brother, but it would be just Kyle and me, sitting in the community center. Surrounded by parents.

The seating is tight and every single one of the folding chairs is occupied, so I'm basically cuddled up next to Kyle, which really, again, could be worse. He doesn't seem to mind. He's not exactly cringing away from me. If anything, he kind of leans in. I can almost imagine that we're back in his basement on my birthday and nothing weird has gone on at all since then.

I lean over a little closer to him, acting like I want to see better when, really, I just want to be close to him for a little while. I miss him so much, and I don't know what to do about it. It's only been four days.

I know that in the end Ruby holds only as much power over me as I let her. That it's not really a big deal. I could come out at any time. But I don't want to come out until I'm ready. This is about me. Not about what information someone has over me.

I also don't want to tell Kyle that I like him until I'm ready. Or maybe I never want to tell him. And while Ruby says she would never out me, and I believe her, I can't be sure that she won't tell Kyle I like him the first chance she gets. She would totally be the kind of person who would tell him in a way that's meant to be like, *Oh, isn't it so cute and funny that Gideon likes you?*

No, Ruby, it's not cute and funny. Because she'd totally be using *cute and funny* as synonyms for *kind of pathetic*.

For a second I worry that I said all of that out loud, because Kyle gets up seemingly out of nowhere, but it's just so he could get a better picture of David being presented his green belt. He even seems to be recording some video to send to Ruby.

David's face totally lights up when he notices Kyle taking pictures of him.

Everyone likes Kyle.

"Where's Ruby?" David asks, flying off the stage after the ceremony is over. "Is Ruby okay?"

"She's fine," Kyle says, pulling him into a quick hug. "She just had to pick Diana up from dance class, so she sent Gideon and me in her place."

"Hey, Gideon," David says.

"Hey, man," I say, giving him a high five. "Your belt looks awesome. I never made it past yellow belt before I quit."

"Thanks," he says, with a big, wide grin.

We stand around and eat some semi-stale cookies while David says good-bye to his classmates and sensei.

"You wanna go get a slice of pizza before we take you home?" Kyle asks as we walk out to his car.

"Yeah, we should do that. We never get to have pizza anymore," David says.

Kyle and I exchange a questioning look over his head but don't say anything.

After pizza and dropping David off, Kyle and I are quiet on our ride home. When we pull into his driveway, we both get out of the car and stand there looking at each other for a second. There are too many things I want to say to him and I don't even know where to start.

"Well," he says.

"Well," I say. "See ya."

"Yeah."

He starts walking up his driveway but then stops and turns around.

"It was weird this week, not talking to you," he says.

"I know," I say, kicking at a rock in the driveway. "I was trying to figure some stuff out."

"What kind of stuff?" Kyle asks, taking a step closer.

I shake my head. "Just stuff." I blink hard because for some reason tears are welling in my eyes. I can't cry just because Kyle asked a question. That would be ridiculous.

"Can you still tutor me?"

I want to say no so bad, because being around him is way harder than I would ever want to admit.

"I'm really nervous about this grade. You know, because of basketball camp this summer. I gotta get my GPA up."

I'm such an asshole.

"Of course," I say. Our friendship needs to be more important than anything else, no matter what. No matter how hard it is to be around him. "Of course I can help you. We'll set up a schedule tomorrow. You'll go to basketball camp."

"Cool," he says with an obvious sigh of relief. "I have that paper due next Friday, and I even know what we need to concentrate on. Ms. Gupta said my last essay relied too much on spell-check and that some of my sentences made no sense."

"You are a terrible speller," I say.

"Yeah? Well, you're short. We all have problems."

I laugh. "I've grown almost half an inch in the past month."

"Sure you have," he says, turning toward his back door. "See ya tomorrow."

"Hey, wait a second," I say, something clicking in my brain. It's April, so there's still plenty of light in the sky even though it's almost dinnertime, and I can see what looks like hope in his expression.

"What's up?"

"I left my mom's car at school," I say, starting to laugh. "I'm such an idiot."

"Oh my God. You fool of a Took."

And for that one brief moment, things feel normal.

eleven

Kyle

After spending time with Gideon yesterday, I feel a little sad or something. I don't really know why. But the fact that he's been trying to figure "stuff" out and hasn't talked to me about whatever stuff it is makes me feel like he's not my best friend anymore.

And then I had another hellish period in English where Ms. Gupta made me read aloud again. After that, she reminded the class that the paper due next week, the one I haven't even started, is 25 percent of our final grade this marking period. Awesome.

When it's finally time to meet up with Ruby by my locker after school, I'm not exactly in the best mood.

"Hey," Ruby says when she sees me. "You look like you just lost your last friend."

I laugh even though it doesn't really sound like a laugh.

"I was just thinking that things with Gideon have been weird lately. They're a little better now, but whatever. No worries."

What sucks is that Ruby looks suspiciously triumphant about the news.

"Maybe you're just growing out of each other," she says.

"We've been friends since we were five. If we were going to grow out of each other, wouldn't that have already happened?"

"Not necessarily. Everyone matures at different rates. Maybe you're maturing faster than Gideon."

I think about that for a second as I spin my lock and go through the motions of getting my homework together.

"But wouldn't it seem like Gideon would grow out of me long before I grew out of him?"

"To look at Gideon, sure, maybe. But I don't think he's as smart and grown-up as he wants everyone to think he is."

"Maybe."

We start walking toward the exit and out to my car.

"I mean, just because he dresses like an old man doesn't mean he really is an old man."

I know I'm supposed to laugh, but I don't. Ruby's joke feels cheap and mean in a way that her jokes usually don't. Ruby can be snarky and sarcastic, but her comments usually come from a place of humor. This comment is obviously meant to tear Gideon down.

She slips her arm through mine.

"Don't worry about it so much. I'm sure you'll be fine

without Gideon around. You'll be way more popular without him, too."

"What?" I ask, scrunching up my nose as we get in the car. "You think our friendship is over? Just like that?" I snap my fingers.

"Maybe, who knows? Now you can be better friends with Buster and those guys. They're more your type anyway."

"Wait, what?" I ask, stopping in the middle of the front hallway.

"You're way cooler than him."

"He's my best friend," I say.

"But it's not like you're married. Friendships change."

"Not with me and Gideon."

"Fine, sorry. I didn't mean to imply that you guys don't have a good friendship. Just that you shouldn't be so down about it. It's not like you don't have any other friends."

She pulls me along toward my car, but I still feel weird and kind of shaken up by what she said. I need to talk to Gideon.

She continues to babble about something that I don't really care about for the ride to her house. More and more lately it feels like Ruby is always talking about something I don't really care about.

Once she's out of the car, I wonder if maybe I'm not growing out of Gideon; maybe I'm growing out of Ruby.

I pull up my driveway and go inside to drop my bag off. Then I come out the back door and hop the fence between our yards before slipping in the sliding door into Gideon's kitchen.

"Hey, Ezra!" I say. He's standing behind the kitchen counter, making the messiest-looking peanut butter and jelly sandwich I've ever seen.

"Hey, Kyle, what's up?"

"Nothing," I say, leaning on the kitchen island. "Is Gideon home?"

"Yeah, he's upstairs. He's in, like, a fortress of despair. Maybe you can make him feel better."

I nod, toss a wave over my shoulder, and head up the stairs.

Gideon

There's a knock on my bedroom door as I lie on my bed, contemplating my next move with Kyle. I avoided him today, but only because I'm torn between coming out to him and giving Ruby too much power. It's a pretty shitty position.

"God, Ma, I told you, I'm fine," I say, striding across the room and then pulling the door open.

"I told you a thousand times I'm not your ma," the person says.

It's Kyle. It's like I summoned him with my thoughts.

"Hey," I say, leaning in the doorway and crossing my arms.

"Hey. Any chance I can come in?"

"Yeah, fine, whatever." I step away from the door and throw myself back down on my bed. Kyle takes a seat in my desk chair, turning it around to face me. Looking at him sitting there, I'm a lot more nervous than I would have expected. Why am I nervous about seeing Kyle? I don't like any of this.

"So, can I help you with something?"

"Yeah, English. Remember? We need to come up with a schedule so that I don't fail out of school."

"You're not going to fail out of school." But then all I can think about is school without Kyle. It's a terrible thought.

We're both quiet for a moment before Kyle takes an audibly deep breath, like he's trying to suck up all the air in the room.

"Are we fighting?" he asks.

"We're not fighting."

"Then what would you call it?" he asks.

"I don't know. We just hung out yesterday."

"But there's something weird between us, right?"

"Jeez, Kyle, I don't know," I say. I hate that he's noticed, too. I didn't want him to notice. I didn't want him to think about how weird I've been recently and then start connecting the dots to the fact that I'm attracted to him.

"You hate Ruby," Kyle says. He states it like it's a fact, like he's trying to catch me off guard.

"I do not hate Ruby," I say, rolling my eyes. Even though I kind of do hate Ruby these days. "Hate is a very strong word."

"Then you hate me," he says, his chin going up like it used to when we were kids and would start fighting. Like he can't control his emotions and his eyes might start tearing up any second.

"Have you considered that maybe this has nothing to do with you?"

"Then what's it about?"

"Maybe I just hate myself."

Kyle's mouth hangs open.

"I don't mean, like I'm—" I start, and stop, sitting up in bed and rubbing my eyes. I really didn't mean to say that. "I don't mean I'm, like, suicidal or something. But I'm trying to figure things out, and maybe I feel like being alone sometimes."

Kyle is still sitting there with his jaw hanging down, not saying anything but looking like I just told him that I started a puppy fight club.

"Or maybe I just *felt* like being alone the past few days. Maybe I'm feeling better."

"Maybe?" he asks.

"I don't know. Life sucks sometimes. There's no explanation. Not really."

"But everything is okay with your family? Are your parents getting divorced?"

"Everything's fine. And no, they're not getting divorced."

"So you just had a lot of feelings and didn't want to talk to me? I mean, I know something's been bothering you lately, but then we hung out yesterday and it seemed like it was better. Like you were better. But then you went back to not talking to me today. I just feel sort of, I don't know, what's the word?"

"Disconnected?" I offer.

"Yeah, disconnected."

"Do you really want to hear about my feelings?" I ask.

He bites his lip and looks out the window, but then he turns back and smiles at me, even though his face is sad and tense. "You can tell me anything."

I suck in a deep breath; he was honest with me about feeling disconnected, so I should be honest with him. "Like I said yesterday, I've been trying to figure some stuff out. And I don't really . . ." I pause, rethinking how I want to present this. "I'm not ready to talk about it yet. But you're my best friend. I promise when I'm ready, you'll be the first to know." *The third to know, technically*, I add silently to myself, since Ruby knows and I accidentally already came out to Ezra.

Kyle nods, and I can see that he's putting on his brave face.

I can't help feeling like there's something he's not saying, too. Maybe I'm just projecting. I study him for another moment before his phone buzzes in his pocket.

He checks it.

"Damn it."

"What's up?"

"It's my mom. I gotta go. But you know you can talk to me anytime, right?" he says.

"Yes."

His phone buzzes again. "Shit."

"What is it?" I ask.

He opens his mouth and shakes his head.

"You know you can talk to me anytime too, right?" I say.

He pinches the bridge between his eyes. "I know."

"So maybe soon we'll both just . . ." I trail off, rolling my eyes at the thought. But then I continue. "We'll both decide to trust each other again."

"Maybe," he says quietly, before backing out of the room.

Kyle

I take a few deep breaths before walking inside my house. The text from my mom said I needed to come home right now because there was a problem.

I go through a list of things that could be wrong. Things like one of my grandparents getting sick, my sisters getting hurt, or maybe my parents are getting a divorce. Maybe I jinxed the divorce thing by asking Gideon about his parents.

I go around in circles with worst-case scenarios for the sixty seconds it takes to get from Gideon's house to my back door.

My parents are sitting in the kitchen waiting for me when I walk in, and I realize how stupid I am. This is about school. How could it be about anything besides school?

It makes me wonder if you can actually lose IQ points. Maybe that time I walked into a stop sign in seventh grade a few of them fell out of my head.

"Kyle," my dad says as I walk in.

"I swear I'll try harder!" I blurt out, interrupting, my anxiety about everything getting the better of me.

"Oh, sweetheart," my mom says. "Have a seat."

I sit.

"I got a call from your English teacher today," my mom says.

I nod, gulping a little for air that seems to have left the kitchen. "I just want to say that I've worked really hard lately in English and I don't know what the problem is, and I think it's probably that Ms. Gupta is out to get me."

"Kyle," she says, her voice containing a note of unexpected warmth and sympathy even as I try to paint my perfectly nice English teacher as a villain. "Ms. Gupta thinks you might have an undiagnosed learning disability."

"She does?" My stomach drops. "I thought I wasn't applying myself or something. I didn't think—I didn't think *that*."

"She called to discuss options with me. We're going to have

a meeting next week with Ms. Gupta, your guidance counselor, and a reading specialist. After that you'll have to take some tests to figure out what's going on. Those tests should be able to provide a clear picture of what kind of problems you might be having."

I'm not as shocked as I would have expected. I think somewhere deep down inside, I've always known that I might be a little bit broken. I just never expected anyone else to notice.

Unfortunately, that thought doesn't help the bubbling anxiety in my stomach as I think about taking these tests.

"But I'm doing okay," I say. "I'm fine."

"Oh, champ," my dad says, calling me *champ* for the first time since I was about eight years old. "Of course you're fine. But maybe if we figure out what kind of obstacles you have, you can find new ways to get past them, rather than banging your head against them over and over."

"Did you ever suspect that something was wrong with me? How has this never come up before?" I feel a little panicked at the thought of what my new reality might look like.

"First of all, nothing is wrong with you," my mom says. "But for the record, I never suspected you had any kind of learning disability, and no one's ever said anything. You always needed a little extra push, but I figured it was because you were a firstborn. You didn't have any brothers or sisters to model yourself after. But nothing's wrong, Kyle. You're not wrong."

"Okay," I say after taking a few more deep breaths.

"It's nothing to worry about," my dad says.

"We're gonna figure this out," my mom promises, patting my hand.

"But you're definitely going to have to come directly home after school and work on your homework. I don't want to see your grades slip any further," my dad adds, before I can feel too good about the conversation. "You still have basketball camp this summer, and I don't want you to jeopardize it."

"So I'm being punished for possibly having a learning disability?" I ask, hearing the whine in my voice and hating it.

"You know that's not what we're doing," my mom says.

They dismiss me after that, probably to talk about me further without me around. But I have to admit that I do feel a little lighter now that things are out in the open. Maybe everything is about to get a little bit easier.

twelve

Gideon

Playing with fire in chem class on a Friday afternoon should never be this boring. I'm not entirely sure why Mrs. Arnold even bothered bringing out the Bunsen burners. There was one thing that needed to be heated up. She could have done it herself and consolidated the flames.

And fine, maybe I'm a little bit scared of fire, but only because my classmates are all obviously morons. I don't know why I decided to take AP Chemistry at the same time as AP Physics. I could have cut way down on my chances of being burned alive. But I just can't help myself. I'm an overachiever.

I spend most of the period sitting alone at the lab table, because my partner is absent. I focus all my energy on thinking about Kyle. It's really helping to distract me from worrying about the school catching on fire.

I still can't stop thinking about my birthday, which feels like a million years ago even though it was just last weekend. And then I go back to Ruby. And Kyle's face when he was in my room yesterday. And then I finish the circle by going back to thinking about my birthday.

What if Kyle likes me, too? He was making almost as much intense eye contact as I was. And it's not like he's homophobic. I don't think that makes sense, to be bisexual and homophobic, but I guess anything is possible.

Furthermore, he's the one who said at the beginning of the marathon that Elijah Wood was cute and then later told me that I remind him of Elijah Wood. If that's not a pickup line, then I have no idea what a pickup line is.

On the other hand, why would he use a pickup line on me?

I have completely lost control over my life. The only thing I can control anymore is the low flame on my Bunsen burner.

I know I need to do something. I need to stop acting like Ruby has some big control over my life, when I know that she doesn't. If I come out to Kyle and tell him I like him, then Ruby has no power over me.

Why does she want power over my life anyway? It's not like I have so much going on. She should concentrate on her own life.

I close my eyes for the briefest of seconds and tell myself that I just need a sign. That something will happen that will set all this in motion. And if I don't get a sign before June, I will definitely tell him over the summer. Or when he gets home from basketball camp. Or definitely before school starts next fall.

Maybe when Ruby leaves for college would be a good time.

Yes. Barring an act of God, I will wait until Ruby is safely installed at college before telling Kyle that I am gay, and in very deep like with him. This news will keep until then.

I happen to open my eyes at the very moment that this girl in my class, Bonnie, passes her lab papers improperly over the flames, and they get singed. She's too dumb to realize they're not actually on fire, so she drops them directly on the burner. Had she simply just thrown them to the side, everything would be fine.

Bonnie's screaming her head off and Mrs. Arnold is running for the classroom emergency gas shutoff and I'm just sitting here stunned, considering that not three minutes ago I was thinking about this very scenario. Perhaps if I've really ruined my life, I can move into a new career as a psychic. I'm already living a fraudulent existence by not coming out of the closet; I could continue the pattern and take people's money in exchange for bogus fortunes.

Mike Maxwell puts the fire out by beating it with Bonnie's backpack, and Bonnie just continues to sit there screaming her head off.

"I saw my whole life flash before my eyes!" she wails. "It was so boring!"

Her friend rubs her back, making cooing noises and trying to get her to calm down.

The next thing I know, Mrs. Arnold is yelling that she can't get the gas off and all the burners flare up higher. I have the distinct feeling that my eyebrows are about to get singed off. I can't stop myself from blocking them with my hands. As if my hands are really going to protect anything during a major gas fire.

The whole class seems to be holding their breath. Even Bonnie finally stopped crying.

"This isn't good," Mrs. Arnold mutters. She runs around to each individual hookup, stopping at mine and trying to turn the connector off. It doesn't seem to have any effect on the flame.

After determining that something is legitimately wrong, she turns to look at us, white-faced. I feel like she's about to apologize or something. It's a very weird moment.

Then she pulls the fire alarm. It starts blaring and we all look at one another, unmoving, as if we still can't believe this is happening.

I'm so scared I can barely move a muscle. Maybe that's what everyone else is feeling, too.

"I'm not kidding, people!" she yells. "We need to get out of here."

Mrs. Arnold grabs her cell phone and calls someone, explaining what just happened while ushering students out of the classroom and into the hallway, where a crowd is building to make their way out of the school.

I think I have my act of God.

I was not expecting that.

Kyle

When the fire alarm goes off during my English class, I'm more than a little relieved. Now I won't get pulled aside by Ms. Gupta at the end of the day. I can look forward to a nice, long

Gupta-less weekend. I really didn't want to share my feelings about the testing she set up for me on Monday. Though she'd already gotten in a few sympathetic smiles before the alarm went off.

During the plodding walk out of the building, it becomes obvious that there are some crazy rumors flying around about why the fire alarm went off. There are a lot of people saying that this isn't just a drill, but it's hard to tell who really knows something and who's just pissing in the wind.

"I heard there were huge flames coming from the science wing," a sophomore in front of me says.

"I heard there was, like, a ball of fire," the kid next to him chimes in.

"Something happened with a gas leak," a girl says, completely separate from the two guys ahead of me.

I'm personally doubtful until a minute later when fire trucks roll onto the street and the teachers start ushering us toward the football field and away from the building.

"That's a first," I mumble. The sophomore turns around and gives me a confused look.

I find Ruby lounging near one of the goalposts with Lauren and Lilah.

"All I'm saying is that we need to find something to do tonight," Lauren says.

"I agree. I can't sit around my house again. I think my parents are starting to feel bad for me. Last Saturday night they asked me to play cards with them. And I did!" Lilah says.

When I sit down next to Ruby, she leans over to kiss my cheek but then jumps back into the conversation.

"I don't have to babysit tonight for once," she says.

"Awesome. All you do lately is babysit," Lauren says.

"Can you hang out tonight?" Ruby asks me.

I nod. "Definitely."

While I'm technically grounded on school nights because of my English grade, Friday is not considered a school night. At least I hope not. I don't know why my parents would make me stay home on Friday night to do my homework when Sunday night is a perfectly reasonable time to get it done.

The girls continue to toss ideas around for what to do that night, and after a few minutes, more of our friends gather in this spot. It seems like everyone is getting comfortable, including the teachers, who are leaning against the fence, watching the fire department activity.

"I guess we're going to be out here awhile," Sawyer says.

"Yeah, something happened with a gas line?" Buster says, but he's obviously not sure about that.

Gideon ambles up, taking a seat between Lilah and Sawyer, but he barely even says hello to anyone.

"Do you know what happened, Gid?" Maddie asks.

"Oh, uh, yeah. Actually, it happened in my chem class."

Everyone grows quiet and all eyes are on Gideon. It gives me an excuse to really look at him for the first time in days. He seems kind of tired and pale. Not words that I've ever used to describe Gideon in the past.

"That's so scary," Lauren says when Gideon's done with his story. "I had no idea that could happen."

"I have a feeling it was a fluke," he says.

The topic turns back to the evening's activities.

"My parents are going to a wedding tonight," Maddie says. "So I'm up for whatever. They won't be home until after midnight."

"Seriously?" Ruby asks. "Maybe we should all go hang out at your house."

"I could probably convince my sister to get us some beer," Buster says.

"This could be a lot of fun," Sawyer says, squeezing Maddie's hand.

"Listen to me," Maddie starts, and she makes direct eye contact with everyone sitting in the group. "I will allow it. But none of you can tell anyone else. This is not a party. This is not about getting wasted. This is not a way for you guys to completely screw me over. It stays between the eight of us. I don't mind having people over. It *will* probably be fun. But if any of you so much as breathes wrong on one of my mother's Hummels or my dad's ships in a bottle, I will cut you."

I glance around the group, and everyone looks about as stunned as I feel.

"This will be an intimate gathering of friends," Maddie says.

"A minute get-together," Lilah says.

"A tiny shindig," Ruby offers.

"So do you want us to take a blood oath?" Buster asks.

Thirty minutes later they finally start letting us back into the school. I feel bad about how quiet Gideon was during the whole fire drill.

I catch up to him as we walk through the front doors and squeeze his arm.

"You're going to come tonight, right?" I ask. I feel like I need him there, but I don't know why.

He looks from my hand to my face. "Yeah, of course. Wouldn't want to miss out on this minuscule nonparty."

"Good. It wouldn't be the same without you."

EZRA

"You look like you just ate a bug," I say.

Gideon is lying on the couch in the family room after dinner, watching TV with a pinched look on his face.

"Why are you still here?" he asks, sitting up to face me.

"Um." I can't believe he asked me that straight out. Not even our parents have asked. No one has asked. Which, come to think of it, is really strange. It's not like I can just tell him that I got evicted and didn't have anywhere else to go.

"No, seriously," he says. "Are you just going to stay here forever?"

"Aren't you happy to have me around?" I ask.

"You're so glib. Why are you so glib?"

"Why do you insist on using SAT words?"

"That's, like, barely an SAT word," he says, throwing himself back down on the couch cushions. "Sorry. I don't mean to be a jerk."

"Yeah, what's your deal? You're so tense lately. Like, way more than usual."

"Everything just really sucks."

"Are people giving you a hard time about the gay thing?" I ask, taking a seat in the chair across from him.

He covers his face with his arm. "No one is giving me a hard time about the gay thing, because no one knows about the gay thing."

"You haven't told anyone?"

He shakes his head.

"I'm the only person who knows?"

He nods. "Essentially. You're the only person I told."

"Well," I say, settling back and probably smiling too much. "I feel pretty special."

"You always feel pretty special," he mutters.

"So you want to tell people?"

He sits up and leans his elbows on his knees. "Yes. But I have this other problem that's really embarrassing."

"Like farting in class embarrassing or boner at the wrong time or . . ." I trail off, because there are so many levels of humiliation.

"Kind of worse than that."

I wait.

"So I'm in love with Kyle."

"Oh. Okay." I steeple my fingers and pretend to be his shrink.

"And I want to tell him. But I also feel like maybe I should tell him I'm gay before I tell him I'm in love with him. You know, like one thing at a time."

I nod knowingly, even though I don't necessarily agree. Gideon just needs support right now.

"So go next door and tell him."

"I love how you make it sound so easy."

"I'm pretty sure it is that easy."

"But what if—"

"No, forget what if," I say, cutting him off. "He's your best friend. He came out to you, you can come out to him."

He takes a noticeably deep breath, like he's trying to calm himself down.

"There's a party tonight. What if I get really drunk and come out to everyone? Get it over with."

I think that sounds like kind of a terrible idea, but I'm trying to be supportive. "Have you ever been drunk before?"

"Um, no."

"It might not be the best idea."

"But it'll be like ripping off a Band-Aid," he says. "And I can kill two birds with one stone. Coming out and getting drunk for the first time."

"I see what you mean. If your life were a teen comedy, tonight would be your night. It would be the climax of your young life."

"Exactly," he says, getting into the idea.

"When are you going to the party?"

He looks at the clock. "I could pretty much leave at any time."

I walk over to our parents' liquor cabinet and grab a bottle. "Here," I say, pouring him a shot glass.

"What is this?" he asks, examining the bottle.

"Liquid courage."

"No, what *is* it?"

"It's called Goldschläger. Just take the shot."

He continues to look at the bottle.

"Drink it and stop dissecting it!" I say. I want to destroy

the evidence before one of my parents comes in to find me giving liquor to their underage son.

"Ach," he says after the shot. "I think I drank the gold."

"I made sure there wasn't any gold in the shot glass."

"There was. I totally drank it," he says, staring into the empty glass. "Am I going to die?"

"Stop being such a square."

He puts the glass down on the liquor cabinet. "Did you just call me a square?"

"Yes. And I meant it."

He laughs.

"And now you need to get to that party."

"Damn straight!" he says, throwing his fist in the air.

"See, I knew the liquor would help."

"I feel all warm and tingly."

"Do you want me to drop you off?" I ask, looking at the glazed expression in his eyes from one shot of Goldschläger.

"Yeah, that'd be good."

thirteen

Gideon

I feel weird as I walk up Maddie's front steps. Extra weird.

I've decided after my conversation with Ezra and my gold-filled shot that I'm going to go with my instincts and get shit-faced drunk tonight. It's on my high school bucket list, and it's definitely not anything I've ever done before. But this seems like a good time to give it a try. My life is kind of in shambles anyway.

I ring the doorbell and Maddie answers a second later.

"Hey, Gideon."

"Hey, Maddie."

I hand her a platter of Rice Krispies Treats.

"You didn't have to bring anything."

"My mom totally insisted when I said I was coming over here. It was easier to let her make them than to argue with her."

"I totally get that."

"I didn't want to raise any suspicions."

"Another good point," she says. "Come on, everyone is out back."

Out back at Maddie's means hanging out on her screened-in porch. It's kind of the perfect night for that.

When she said everyone, she meant everyone. I'm the last person to arrive, which immediately makes me feel like everyone was talking about me before I got here.

That's a terrible feeling.

They greet me with various levels of enthusiasm. I honestly don't think I'd be here right now if Kyle hadn't pulled me aside to make sure I was going to come tonight. But I have no backbone when it comes to him. At least not anymore.

I take the last seat at the table between Buster and Sawyer.

"Do you want a drink, Gideon?" Maddie asks.

"Um, yeah. I guess just a beer is fine."

"And Gideon's mom made Rice Krispies Treats," she says, placing them at the center of the table.

Buster makes a mad grab for one. "Are there M&M's in there?"

I shake my head.

"That's cool, still delicious."

"Yeah, sorry I couldn't get ahold of any booze," I say, even though if I'd been thinking more clearly I probably could have convinced Ezra to stop and buy some on the way over here.

He seemed more invested in my social life than I ever would have guessed possible.

"No worries, we have plenty," Ruby says, nodding at the folding table set up behind me. There are three or four different liquors along with a bunch of different mixers, and underneath is an ice chest with beer.

"That's a lot for just eight of us," I say, picking up a beer.

"Well, better get drinking," Buster says, slapping my knee.

I take a sip of my beer and almost spit it out. "This is—"

"Not the best," Kyle says. "We know. But it was cheap and it was all Buster's sister was willing to get us, because we didn't have enough money for anything decent."

"And she refused to chip in even a couple bucks."

"I could have given you guys some money."

"Now you tell us," Buster says. "Just chug it real fast."

"Or I'll drink it. I don't mind," Kyle says. I hand him the bottle and he takes a long pull. My mind instantly goes to the fact that his lips are touching where my lips just touched.

"You want to try something awesome?" Ruby asks.

"Like what?"

"I like to call it National Velvet. It's amaretto and Dr. Pepper."

"Sounds smooth," I say. And it is. It tastes like candy and instantly makes me feel a little warmer, a little happier. I know that I'm not drunk yet, even with the shot of Goldschläger I took at home, but it's nice to feel something else besides kind of bored and sort of sad. Those have been my go-to emotions lately.

Half the people at the table are playing poker, but the other half are just watching and chatting idly; it's kind of nice.

I drink my first National Velvet fast and get up for another.

"Have you ever been drunk before, Gideon?" Ruby asks. She's standing at the booze table, mixing a drink for herself.

"Definitely not," I tell her.

"You want another one?"

"Hell yes," I say, handing over my cup to her. "I want to get drunk tonight. It seems like a good idea. You know, since I never have been. And I can just walk home from here. I don't have to worry about getting lost or anything."

"I think you might already be a little tipsy," she says, handing me back my cup.

"I feel a little warm," I say, making more intense eye contact than I really mean to. "My brother gave me a shot of something with gold chunks in it before I left the house."

She laughs but then turns away from me. For a second I forgot that we're in a standoff.

I notice Kyle gets up to go to the bathroom. A few seconds later, when nobody's paying attention, I decide to follow him. I lurk in the hallway outside and try not to listen to him pee.

"Listen, Kyle," I say when he walks out of the bathroom. "You know, I just want everything to be okay between us."

"Everything's fine between us."

"But you left my house so fast yesterday. And I wanted to bring it up at school today, but I wasn't sure how personal it was, and I didn't want to bring up bad news. I should have texted you. I'm such a terrible friend."

"Gideon, it's fine. If it was a big deal, don't you think I would have told you about it?"

"I guess," I say, taking a step back and stumbling into the wall.

"How much did you drink, Gid?"

"Two National Velvets. And Ezra gave me a shot. How much did you drink?"

"Just your beer."

"You should drink more, Kyle. It's delicious."

"I'll take that into consideration."

He walks away before I have a chance to say what I wanted to say. Which is not a bad thing, since I can't remember what I wanted to tell him in the first place. Alcohol makes my brain very mixed up.

I sit down in Maddie's kitchen and watch the clock tick away minutes for a little while, trying to remember what I wanted to tell Kyle. When I go back out onto the porch, everyone seems almost as drunk as I feel.

"Hey, hey," I say when I get back out there. "Were you guys talking about me while I was gone?"

"Nope," Lauren says. "But you look like you want another drink."

"I think I do. I think I really do."

Ruby

Gideon seems well on his way to drunk, and Kyle is catching up slowly on beer.

I'm mostly pretending to be drunk, because it's fun that way. And I didn't want to be drunk for what I'm about to propose.

"Oh my God," I say, standing up to get everyone's attention. "I have the best idea, guys. It is the best idea ever!"

"What?" Maddie asks, sipping something pink with a straw.

"Truth or dare. We should totally play truth or dare."

"That is such a good idea, Ruby," Lilah says, crunching on a pretzel stick and then accidentally biting her finger.

"Oh, oh!" Sawyer says. "I know how we should play. My cousin taught me this way where each round, everyone writes down one truth and one dare and then you put them in two bowls and people pick."

This is not going the way I expected it to. I was going to have all the control of the game as the only sober person playing, but now there's this other element. I can't manipulate the game, or drunk Gideon. I really want him to get all his secrets out in the open. The whole situation is starting to bore me—in part because Gideon's too smart to really play around with.

I consider vetoing this idea.

Oh, screw it. Truth or dare will be fun no matter what.

"Is it better that way?" Lauren asks.

"Well, yeah. Because you might end up getting your truth or dare, but no one will know if you put in a really hard one. There's strategery," Sawyer says.

"Strategery?" Maddie asks, snorting.

"Oh, you know what I mean."

"I'll go get some bowls," Maddie says.

"And some paper and some pens!" Sawyer calls after her.

Maddie comes back a minute later, and we all gather around the table to write down our truths and dares.

"All right, Buster goes first, and we'll move around the table this way," I announce as we settle down for our game.

Buster picks up the dare bowl. I don't think anyone is all that surprised.

"'Lick the floor,'" he reads. "Cool."

"Wait, wait, wait," Lauren says as Buster's about to lick the all-weather tile on the porch. "What happens if we don't accept the dare or the truth? What's the punishment?"

"I was going to accept the dare!" Buster says.

"I know, I know, honey," she says, patting his butt. "But this is stuff we need to work out before we get into the game."

"Okay, well," I say, since apparently I'm the master of ceremonies tonight. "If you don't take the dare or you won't answer the question truthfully, you have to let Buster put makeup on you."

"That sounds awful," Lilah says.

"That's the point."

"I want to put makeup all over all your faces," Buster says from the floor. He takes a big old lick and then gets back into his chair. Then he pours himself a shot of amaretto and takes it back. "That stuff is awesome. It tastes like delicious cough medicine."

"I know, man," Gideon says, smiling with all his teeth. Gideon has been in a particularly good mood this evening. I think he was slightly drunk when he showed up. He doesn't even look scared of me anymore.

"Lilah, you're up."

She grabs for the dare bowl, too. These people are crazy. Always go with truth.

"'Sniff everyone's armpits,'" she reads. "That's gross. But you guys all look pretty clean."

"Both arms," I tell her for good measure.

She starts with her own and then works her way around the table, pausing longest at Maddie.

"Hmm. What is that? I like that," Lilah says.

"According to Secret, that's what Australia smells like, because that's what the scent is called."

"Where'd you get it?"

"Walgreens."

"Nice, nice," Lilah says as she drifts around the circle, giving everyone's armpits a hearty sniff before getting back to her seat. "I would like to thank you all for being good-smelling, clean people. Especially Maddie. And you too, Gideon. You got a good thing happening over there. You smell like my dad."

"Is that really a good thing?" he asks, his voice a little hard to understand since he's chewing determinedly on a straw.

"I like it," Lilah says with a smile. She passes the bowls to Lauren, who reinforces the fact that we're kindred spirits by grabbing for a truth.

"'If you were the opposite sex for a day, what is the first thing you would do?'" she reads. "That's easy: pee standing up."

"Wow, you were really prepared for that question," Sawyer says.

"I have five brothers," she says simply. "It's always been a dream of mine."

"Moving on," I say, passing the bowls to Maddie.

Maddie studies both of them for a moment and then, in the surprise of the night, reaches for a dare.

"Either way it's terrifying, but I think I'd rather *do* something than confess something." She sucks in a breath and unfolds the slip of paper. "'Dump glitter over your head while singing "Glitter in the Air" by Pink.'"

"Oh man, that's mine," Buster says delightedly.

"I'm sorry. I can't do that. It's just way too much of a mess.

My parents are going to be home in, like, two hours and glitter lasts forever. I'll take my punishment."

"Actually, I think you have the power of veto on this," I say. "We should have laid out that rule beforehand, but I can't force you to make a mess when you've been supercool. You okay with that, Buster?"

He nods. "I didn't think about how hard it would be to clean up. I just thought it sounded really funny. And I like that song."

"No worries," Maddie says. "I really will let you do my makeup."

"Nah, just take another dare."

Maddie reads the next one. "'Take a shot of vodka with Tabasco in it.' That is terrifying. But I'll do it."

A few minutes later there's a shot glass in front of her.

"This is going to set my mouth on fire," she says. "Like, instead of internal bleeding, won't I have internal burns? I should chase it with milk."

"I've done it," I tell her, but I run to pour her a glass of milk anyway. "You'll be fine."

She sucks it down and then slams the glass back on the table. "Oh God, the vodka is so much worse than the Tabasco."

Everyone laughs, and then it's Sawyer's turn. He picks truth because he's smart and just has to answer the longest he's gone without showering. "This is, like, such a not-fun answer, but three days while I was camping last summer. I feel like I should take another one."

"No worries, there will be plenty of rounds to come," I say, reaching to take a truth and reading it out loud. "'What's the last lie you told?'"

I look around the table.

"I'm sorry, Maddie, but I've never taken a Tabasco shot. I just didn't want you to be nervous."

She looks exultant. "O-M-G! I can't believe this. I feel like the coolest kid ever now for taking that shot." She gets up to hug me. "Thanks for lying. I feel like that time Pam Beesly walked on hot coals on that episode of *The Office*."

"You are totally like Pam Beesly," Sawyer says, giving her a kiss on the cheek.

It's hard not to smile around those two.

And then it's Kyle's turn. He grabs for a dare, shocking the hell out of me.

"A dare?" I ask, raising an eyebrow at him. "I feel like I don't even know you anymore."

"I'm a whole new man," he says, unfolding the paper.

Kyle

I read the dare through several times, making sure that it isn't just my poor reading skills trying to fool me.

Kiss the person you want to kiss the most in this room.

"I'll take the punishment," I say, shoving the slip of paper into my pocket.

"Seriously?" Ruby asks, her eyes bugging out of her face.

"Yeah, I don't want to do that dare. I'm not comfortable with it."

"What is it?" Buster asks.

"I don't think there's a rule that I have to tell the group what the dare is. I'm just allowed to skip it."

Ruby studies me closely, and I'm worried that she knows

what the dare is. Maybe it was her dare and she was trying to check on my loyalties. Maybe she knows I like Gideon. Maybe she knows that lately I've been thinking about breaking up with her to date him. Because I kind of can't stop thinking about him.

Maddie gets some makeup for Buster to put on me, and then it's Gideon's turn.

He grabs a truth and reads it out loud. "'What is the biggest secret you're currently keeping?'"

Buster is having a really good time with the eye shadow and then starts in on some lipstick.

"Um," Gideon says. He wraps his fingers around the arms of his chair. "Um. Well. Um. You guys are my friends, right?"

Everyone nods, including me. It's harder than you might expect, because Buster has my head in a vise grip.

"Stop fidgeting," Buster says. "You're going to mess up your face."

"You're already messing up my face," I mutter.

"So, I'm gay."

"You're what?" I ask, leaning out of Buster's grip and getting a long line of lipstick across my cheek.

"Gay," Gideon repeats. "I am gay. And I've never actually told anyone before, except my brother, Ezra, but apparently amaretto makes me chatty."

"Thanks for telling us, Gid," Ruby says, patting his arm. She looks almost as relieved as Gideon does.

"Yeah, I'm sorry it had to come from a dumb game, but we're all happy for you," Maddie says.

Sawyer pats him on the back, and Buster practically tackle-hugs him.

"Woo-hoo," Lilah says, but I'm not sure she even knows what's really going on at this point. I'm pretty sure she was taking a nap.

"To Gideon," Lauren says, raising her mostly empty glass.

He's smiling so hard, and they all look so happy for him. Everyone raises their glass and we knock them all together. Except me.

This should be good news. I should be happy for Gideon, too. He's a good guy. He's my best friend. But I can't shake this terrible feeling in my gut, like he's been hiding this from me for some reason.

I get up without a word and go out the front door, leaving it open a crack because I don't want it to lock behind me. I just need a minute to sit by myself on the front steps and collect my thoughts. Drinking four beers was a bad idea. My brain is mushy and refuses to focus. It's kind of how I feel when I have to read in class.

Feet shuffle behind me, and I know it's Gideon. There's no way anyone else would have the balls to follow me. Not right now. Not even Ruby.

Gideon hands me some tissues.

"I'm not crying."

"No, but you do have lipstick all over your face."

"Oh, right," I say, as I start wiping away whatever Buster did to me.

"What's wrong?" Gideon asks after several minutes of quiet. He sits next to me but leans far away, taking up as little room as possible on the other end of the step. He crosses his arms and folds at the waist, huddling over his legs and not looking at me.

I shake my head. I don't know where to start. "Nothing. Everything."

"I'd kind of hoped we'd bond over this," he says. "You know, you're bi, I'm gay. They could make a reality show about us on Bravo or something."

He's still not looking at me, and I don't know if I want him to. I close my eyes and try to chase down a coherent thought in my muddled brain.

"Why didn't you trust me?" I ask.

"I trust you," he says, looking over at me. His eyes are startled in the harsh glow of the front porch light.

I clear my throat and level my gaze at him. "It kind of seems like you don't, since you didn't tell me about being gay."

"It seems weird that you of all people would say that, considering the hard time Ruby gave you when you came out to her."

He's kind of got me there. "Oh right," I say, staring at the sidewalk.

"I didn't tell anyone. Except Ezra."

"Why not?"

"Maybe I just wasn't ready. Maybe I'm not as comfortable in my own skin as you are. We can't all be as lucky as bisexual poster child Kyle Kaminsky."

"I'm not that comfortable," I say, wiping my sweaty palms on my jeans.

"I just wasn't ready," he says. "I was waiting for something. A moment where I felt like everything was clear."

"How long have you known?"

"I guess I've always kind of suspected. But I never wanted to deal with it. It wasn't denial or internalized homophobia.

Kind of just being scared to figure out who I was and place a label on it. Also the fact that I didn't want to waste time on this crap in high school."

I can't help but laugh, because that's Gideon in a nutshell.

"So what changed?"

He swallows a few times, his Adam's apple bobbing. He's nervous. Something's making him nervous, and I think it's me.

"Did I do something?" I ask.

He glances over at me, squinting. "Kind of but not really. I just noticed one day, not that long ago, how jealous I was of you and Ruby. And it all kind of hit me. Like really hit me. Hard, in the gut, over and over again."

"You were jealous?"

"So jealous," he says, shaking his head. "I still am."

"Because you like me?" I ask. I think that's what he's saying, but it's hard to believe.

"I mean, um, yeah. Amaretto must be some kind of truth serum."

"You *like* like me?"

"Well, yeah. I'm sorry. I don't want to weird you out. We don't have to talk about this anymore."

"This just seems kind of sudden. You're gay, and you like me. I'm taking it all in." What I don't add is the fact that I like him. I know I should say it out loud, but I'm not there yet. I wish I were the kind of person who could say things like that spontaneously. Maybe if I had a few minutes to plan it out. I never imagined this happening tonight. Or ever really.

I never expected Gideon to be gay.

I also know that if I tell him I like him, I might try to kiss him, and I really don't want to be the kind of guy who cheats on his girlfriend with his best friend.

No matter how cute Gideon is.

"It's not really all that sudden to me. And I'm pretty drunk," he says, and then he smiles goofily. "I pulled my shit together to talk to you, but damn, everything is a little spinny."

"Do you want to go back inside?"

"Honestly? No. I feel like this night can only go downhill from here."

"I'll walk home with you," I say.

"You sure?"

I nod. Of course I'll walk him. I'd probably walk with him anywhere.

I promise myself I'll start saying these things out loud to him. As soon as my hands stop shaking.

We start walking in the direction of our houses, slowly. Gideon stumbles a few times and I take his arm. It feels like there's an empty desert between us, and I don't know what might be waiting to bite my foot with one wrong step. Or maybe that's the beer talking. I don't know. I've never actually been this drunk before, and I don't even really think I'm that drunk.

Our hands brush together a couple of times and, oh man, I want to hold his hand so bad but I don't know how he'd react. Except that he admitted he liked me. I finally work up the courage to grab for it on the last block. I need him to know that we're good, and that was the best way to show him.

We get to his house first and I walk him to the back door, where we stand on his deck for a minute.

"I guess this is it," he says.

But it isn't. Not really. I don't know how to tell him that until I remember the slip of paper in my pocket. I fish it out and hand it to him. This is a good way to say everything I want to say.

"'Kiss the person you want to kiss the most in this room,'" he reads.

I'm still holding his hand. I don't know that I've ever actually held his hand for this long. Friendship is kind of a stupid, arbitrary thing when you think about it. You should be able to hold your friend's hand whenever you want. How is holding hands more intimate than giving a hug? Who makes those decisions?

"So who was it?" he asks, looking up at the moon.

I examine his profile. "Who do you think?"

We hold eye contact for way too long, and he opens and closes his mouth a few times.

I can't stop glancing at his lips. I need to leave before I do something I'll regret.

"I have to go," I tell him.

Before he can answer, I fly off the deck and hop over the fence without looking back.

Gideon

It's probably a good thing he left, because I really wanted to kiss him.

fourteen

Kyle

I wake up before dawn on Saturday morning, and my head feels like it's made out of rocks. No, something worse than rocks. I don't even have the brain capacity to figure out what it feels like it's made of, so I'll just leave it at rocks for now.

But, oh man, I have to pee. I have to pee so bad I can't think about anything else. I get out of bed and have to stand still for a second before stumbling toward the door and opening it, squinting out into the dim hallway before remembering which direction the bathroom is in.

I slide back into bed as soon as possible, and when I wake up again, it's three hours later and something's bothering me.

I squeeze my eyes shut tight against the thoughts assaulting my tired brain.

Gideon.

Gideon and I had a moment.

A much bigger moment than the one we had on his birthday.

He told me he liked me. Did I tell him I like him too? I can't remember—it's all kind of a blur.

But I really wanted to kiss him. More than I've ever wanted to kiss anyone in my entire life.

I groan and pull the covers over my head, even though I know I'm not going to be able to fall back to sleep again. Not when the full reality of what happened last night has hit me head on.

The worst part is that I'm actually happy about it. I'm happy that I had a moment with Gideon.

This isn't right.

I'm better than this.

I glance over at my phone. That might hold some of the answers I need this morning, but I'm not sure I'm ready to deal with the reality of it. It could also hold bad news.

I decide to take a shower, trying to scrub off all this lingering guilt. Of course that doesn't work, and basically I'm just left with skin that feels like it's been rubbed raw. Kind of like my outsides match my insides today.

When I get down to the kitchen, I find a note taped to the fridge saying that my mom took my sisters shopping.

I try to eat some cornflakes, but they turn into paste in my mouth. I drink a lot of water and avert my gaze from Gideon's house next door. I can't even look at it without feeling like a complete dickhead.

I need to man up. I need to talk to Ruby.

I pull up in front of her house without so much as a text to warn her I was coming. I sit there for a minute, trying to figure out what exactly I'm going to say to her. I probably should have checked my phone before I left the house. Ruby's not the kind of girl who appreciates people dropping by out of nowhere.

While I'm working up the courage to get out of the car, Ruby slips through her front door and ambles to the car.

I guess this is really going to happen.

"Well, if it isn't my boyfriend," she says, slumping into the passenger seat.

"How did you know I was here?"

"Just happened to look out the window." She yawns and rubs her eyes. "I'm not exactly surprised to see you here."

"I did something."

"Yeah, you came to my house before noon on a Saturday."

"I did something bad."

I take a deep breath, and she looks over at me expectantly. When I don't continue she says, "Lemme guess. You kissed Gideon." She laughs a little.

"No, but I wanted to," I say. I take a deep breath. "I'm so sorry. I wish I had words to explain how sorry I am."

"Why are you apologizing? You didn't actually do any-thing." She seems confused with the whole conversation and really just not getting what I'm trying to say.

"Listen, Ruby," I start. It must be my tone of voice, because things seem to click into place for her.

"Holy crap, you're going to break up with me for Gideon!"

"Yeah, I think I have to."

"I thought you actually liked me," she says.

"I did. I do. It was a spur-of-the-moment feeling. Mostly because of that stupid dare," I explain.

"What was the dare?" she asks. "Why were you so weird about it?"

"It said to kiss the person in the room that you want to kiss the most. And my beer-addled logic wouldn't let me lie and just kiss you. I didn't expect Gideon to come out, like, five seconds after I thought about kissing him. It was all a lot to take in."

"How long have you liked him?" she asks.

"I don't know. It's just kind of been lurking in the back of my head recently, but I didn't even know he was gay."

"This just sucks, Kyle."

"I'm so sorry, Ruby."

"What am I supposed to say to that? What am I supposed to do about this?"

"I don't know, I'm just trying to be honest with you."

"So, what, you want me to thank you for coming over here and being honest or something?"

"All I know is that I don't want to cheat on you, so I came here to tell you what's up."

"You're really going to break up with me for Gideon."

I nod. It's like she's so shocked she doesn't believe me. But I can see it starting to dawn on her face that this is real.

She takes a deep breath, and I steel myself for whatever comes next. "Fine. But I'm going to tell everyone I broke up with you. They'll believe it and it will keep my image intact."

"I had no idea you cared that much about your image."

She pulls down the sun visor to look at herself in the mirror, but her hair isn't done and she's not wearing any makeup, so she just slams the visor shut and turns back to me.

"I've been talking to Josh Barton a lot recently."

"Um, good for you."

"Just so you don't think you're the only person with someone on deck."

I can see in her face and hear in her voice that she's trying to cover up that I hurt her by talking about all this other crap. But I've gotten to know her really well, and she can't fool me. She's just lucky I'm too nice a guy to call her out. Doesn't mean I have to be nice about Josh Barton.

"Didn't he get left back, like, three times?" I ask. Not that I'm in any place to judge someone else's academic standing, but I need to fight back a little bit.

"Only once in high school," she says. "And then, like, kindergarten or something that doesn't really matter. He might not be the smartest guy, but I know for sure he's not going to break up with me for Gideon Berko."

"Okay, sure. Yeah, whatever," I say, running my hands around the steering wheel.

"Just one other thing," she says. "When did you stop liking me?"

It's so weird that she can go from angry, image-driven Ruby one second to just a normal person with insecurities the next.

"I didn't stop liking you. I just started to like Gideon more. You can't control that kind of stuff, you know?"

She looks like she might cry now. I really don't want her to cry.

"Well, it's been real, Kyle Kaminsky. Thanks for everything."

With that, she gets out of the car and runs up her front steps, letting the door slam behind her so hard that it shakes the front of the house.

She doesn't look back.

Five minutes later I pull into my driveway, happy to see that I beat my mom and my sisters home. I run inside and throw away the note I left, exchanging it for one that says I'm at Gideon's. Normally I would text my mom, but I'm still not ready to face whatever might be on my phone from last night. Including what I'd imagine are some pretty incriminating pictures of me getting a makeover from Buster before everything else happened.

Before I even look at it, I need to talk to Gideon.

Ruby

I stomp up my front steps and slam the door behind me, making the family portraits on the wall rattle. I slam it again and one of the frames actually falls down.

I still don't feel better.

I lost my boyfriend to Gideon Berko. I am the lowest of the low on the totem pole. He's not even on the totem pole, and yet he stole Kyle away from me without even trying. He didn't even have to kiss Kyle to make Kyle realize how much he preferred Gideon over me.

Regret flares up like lightning. I should have taken Gideon down when I had the chance.

I hope he truly appreciates and comprehends the favor I did him by never showing anyone those lists he made. But he's so full of himself he hasn't even brought them up again. He never even asked me about them. Like, how much of an ego do you have to have to not worry about someone having such personal information?

But I guess now that he's out and going to start dating Kyle, he doesn't see the damage I could do with that list.

I could sit back and watch his world burn.

I totally could. I could make life miserable for Gideon Berko.

It's the only comfort I have at this point.

Gideon

I hear Kyle's footsteps on the deck, and my first instinct is to hide. I sink down into the couch cushions. The back door is locked, so when he jiggles the handle, Ezra goes to let him in. Kyle asks if I'm home, and Ezra tells him I'm in the family room.

There's literally nowhere to hide, so I scrunch myself deeper in the sofa and pretend I didn't hear anything.

"Was that the pizza?" I ask, showing off what an excellent actor I am.

"No, I'm not pizza," Kyle says, shoving his hands into his pockets.

"Hey," I say, trying to stand up casually and failing. I get all tangled up in the afghan and almost fall over the coffee table. "I am perfectly fine and totally normal."

"You're blushing."

"Yes. Yes I am." I try to regain my footing, but either I'm still very hungover or just the mere sight of Kyle has thrown me completely off balance.

He takes a step toward me and leans his hip on the easy chair next to the couch. We're within five feet of each other, but it's like I can feel all the emotions rolling off him.

"So about last night," he says.

"I'm so sorry," I say.

"You don't have to apologize. What do you think you have to be sorry for?"

"I don't even know. I guess that I made you question whether I trust you or not. I definitely trust you. Completely. One hundred percent."

"I trust you, too," he says.

I bob my head. "Cool, cool. Glad we got all that out of the way."

"How are you feeling today?" he asks, sitting on the arm of the chair. If my mom were here, she'd yell at him. Why am I thinking about my mom?

"Like I drank way too many National Velvets last night," I say.

"Is this what a hangover is?"

"I don't know. But according to Ezra, I'll feel better if I drink a lot of water and take some Advil. He also ordered a pizza for me, even though it's not even noon yet. He says the grease has magical properties."

"So why don't you do that? At least the water and Advil part, while you wait for your magical pizza?" he asks.

"I don't know, I feel like this is my punishment. Like I deserve this for the sins I committed last night."

"You didn't commit any sins."

"Pretty sure I was coveting my neighbor's wife."

"Except Ruby's not your neighbor."

"Fine, but you know what I mean," I say, rolling my eyes.

"And I'm not her wife anymore."

"That fast?"

"Yeah, I went over there to break up with her this morning," he says with a barely contained grin.

"Cool." I crack my knuckles and look around the room. I have no idea what to say, because suddenly everything I've wanted for the past month is coming true. I guess that fire in chem lab really was the sign I needed. "My parents are out for a couple more hours. Do you want to stay and hang out? Watch some TV?"

He closes the distance between us and I think he's going to sit down, but instead he looks at me like he's never seen me before. I'm really glad I brushed my teeth.

Our faces are close.

"What happens now?" he asks.

"I don't know. I've never seen this episode."

"No, I mean with us," he says, smiling.

"Oh." I glance away. "I guess we'll find out."

He chews his lip, and all I can think about is kissing him. It's been building up inside of me for months, and I just know I need to get it out of my system. I need to go for it. I want to sit next to him on the couch, and I want our knees to touch. I want to remember that everything that happened last night and everything we said was real.

I put my hand on the back of his neck and pull him close, standing on my tiptoes to press my lips to his. It's quick and dry and maybe not the most romantic or centered kiss that has ever passed between two people.

But it's our first, and I immediately know that I don't want it to be our last.

fifteen

Kyle

I spend most of the day on Sunday with my family, trying to get back on my parents' good side after the whole English grade thing from the other day. I'm not technically grounded on weekends, but it seemed like they weren't so much asking me to go to the movies with the family, as telling me I had to go along with them.

By the time I get home from family fun day, I'm sort of desperate to see Gideon. I don't even bother going into my house before hopping the fence.

He's sitting on his deck, reading a book. He doesn't notice me at first, and I have this moment where I want to turn around and go home. I shove my hands into my pockets and swallow that feeling away. It's Gideon. I like Gideon. A lot. In all different ways.

"*The Great Gatsby*," I say, ambling up the deck steps and squinting at the title.

He shades his eyes in the glowing afternoon sun and looks at the book cover as if surprised to see that's what he has in his hands.

"Yeah, I figured if I'm going to help you with your English paper this week, I need to refresh my memory on this book."

He slips a bookmark between the pages before lifting his feet off the patio chair he had them propped on and offering it to me. I sit down and lean all the way back, feeling jittery and out of place.

This is where I should tell him what's going on with the whole learning disability issue, but I have it stuck in my head that Gideon isn't going to like me anymore once he finds out that I have this *thing*. Gideon is so smart. It's not like he's unaware that I've always been behind him in school. This isn't some big secret.

I promise myself that I'll tell him what's going on as soon as it has a real name and definition. It'll be easier to talk about.

"Um, don't worry too much about the tutoring," I say. "I'll let you know if I need help. Gupta's trying something else with me first, but I don't really know if it's going to work out." I don't really want to tell him what's happening until I know for a fact that something *is* happening.

"Okay, well, let me know," he says, shrugging. "What's up?"

Words lodge in my throat. I planned a whole speech while I was out today and now the words have all disappeared.

"You look like you're going to pass out," he says, obviously trying to make a joke, as I really do feel like I might pass out.

I barely even hear him, because the words that I wanted to say are finally tumbling out of my mouth.

"Do you want to go on a date? With me? Next weekend?" I spit out the question and then have to take a deep breath to steady myself. A weird nervous shiver goes through my whole body. "I would say we should go during the week but I'm not allowed out on school nights until my grades get better."

Gideon licks his lips, which is good because now I'm thinking about kissing him instead of the slow death by embarrassment that might be coming my way if he says no.

"I've been thinking about this a lot," he says.

"Yeah, me too."

"You really want to date me? Like, we're best friends—what if we ruin everything?"

"You're really worried about that?"

"Yes," he says, his voice firm and sure in a way that mine never is.

"I would hope that we're good enough friends that we kind of know what we're getting ourselves into. It's not like dating you is going to be some big shocking difference. We already spend a lot of time together."

"What about when you and I leave for college? What then?"

"Oh, come on, Gideon. That's, like, way over a year from now. Why are you even thinking like that? What about all the fun we could have between now and then?"

"We are going to have fun," he says.

"Hell yeah." I squeeze his knee.

I lean forward in my chair, finally feeling relaxed about the whole exchange, even if he still hasn't given me a firm yes about going out on a date.

"And you're sure Ruby is okay with all this?" he asks.

"Yes. Definitely. She told me that she's going to tell everyone that she broke up with me, but what do I care?"

"She's a little bit crazy," he says.

"Maybe a little. I try not to judge. She's got an image to uphold, apparently."

His face cracks into the realest non-drunk smile I've seen from him in a long time.

"So, what do we do?"

"Well, first you probably have to say whether or not you want to go on a date with me someday. Don't leave a guy hanging."

"What's this someday business? I thought you said next weekend?"

I frown at him.

"Fine, yes, I get what you're saying," he says, rolling his eyes. "I would like to go on a date with you next weekend."

"Awesome."

"But, like, are you . . ." He pauses and squeezes his eyes shut like the embarrassment of asking this question is too much to take. "Are you my boyfriend?"

"Only if you're mine," I say.

He leans his head back and smiles at the sky. "Obviously."

I move my chair so we're sitting next to each other instead of across from each other. "I also think we should kiss again sometime. Maybe."

He side-eyes me. "Oh, I get it. You're just here for these sweet, sweet lips." He points at his mouth.

"You're an idiot."

"You're a bigger idiot."

He shifts in his chair, turning his body toward me, and then licks his lips again. I mirror him, right down to the lip licking.

When he presses his lips to mine this time, it's different—not rushed, not too dry. It feels like we're teaching each other something that we don't have words for.

I turn my head a little to the side, and he sucks in a deep breath. He leans his forehead against mine.

"You okay?" I ask.

"That was, like, way better than last time."

"Yeah, it'll probably get even better the more we do it."

"I can't wait," he says, leaning back in for more.

Gideon

Kyle and I spend the better part of an hour making out on my deck. If I wasn't worried about my parents coming home any second, I would totally bring him up to my room because believe me, having those chair arms between us was the worst thing that ever happened in the history of making out.

"Mom called to say she's bringing home Chinese food,"

Ezra says, sticking his head out of the sliding door and ruining our fun. "Oh, hey there, Kyle. I didn't know you were here."

"He was just leaving," I say, pushing on his arm as if I could throw him over the fence before my brother says anything too embarrassing. Hopefully, he'll take the hint.

"No, I wasn't," Kyle says, pouting.

"I hear you broke up with Ruby Vasquez for Giddyup."

"Um," Kyle says. But before he can even answer, Ezra continues.

"Was that really the best idea? That chick is hot. She was a freshman when I was a senior," he explains.

"'Cause that doesn't make you sound like a creep," I mutter.

Kyle scratches at the back of his neck and sighs, but at least he's smiling. He's very familiar with Ezra's ridiculousness. "You know, she ended up breaking up with me, actually."

"She's smart. Getting rid of the deadweight," Ezra says, punching Kyle in the shoulder playfully. Then he sits in one of the other chairs. I groan when Kyle settles back down.

"So, what are you still doing here?" Kyle asks.

"Isn't that the ultimate question?" Ezra asks. "Who put us here? What is our earthly purpose?"

Kyle rolls his eyes and I sigh. "I guess you're going to stick around for a while?"

"Indefinitely," Ezra says.

Kyle's phone buzzes in his pocket and he takes a quick peek. "I gotta get out of here. I'm not technically supposed to be socializing, since it's a school night."

I stand with him and grab his arm, planting one last hard kiss on his lips, in part because I can't stop myself, but also because for some reason I feel the need to flaunt this new relationship in front of Ezra. He always had girls around. Now it's my turn to have this boy around. This very cute boy.

Kyle leaves, and I turn my attention to my brother.

"So, that's new," he says.

I nod.

"What's the deal?"

"Um, well, we're dating. He came over to ask me on a date."

"Where are you going?"

"Actually we never decided that part," I say. "We'll figure it out."

"Well, good for you," Ezra says. "You gonna tell Mom and Dad someday?"

I take a deep breath. "Soon."

"Take your time. But you know they're gonna be okay with it, right?"

"I keep telling myself that."

"Well," he says, standing up and patting my shoulder, "I'm telling you that, too."

"Thanks."

"Just let me know when you're going to do it, so I can record Mom's overly delighted reaction and make myself famous with the viral video entitled 'Woman Loses Her Shit in a Good Way.'"

I'm trying to think of a comeback, but he's already inside, turning the TV on to whatever reality show marathon he can find. Ezra loves reality shows.

sixteen

Ezra

"So you're really going to tell them tonight, right?" I ask, barging into Gideon's room a few nights later and sitting on his bed. We're going out for dinner for our mom's birthday.

He's standing at his closet, looking at the same exact clothes he wears every day and acting like he's going to find something new in there.

"Yeah," he squeaks, sounding like someone just grabbed his balls.

"That's awesome. I think it's time." Perhaps my unyielding support will help with the ball-grabbing situation.

"They're not even gonna care, right?" he asks, turning to look at me, his face just as pinched as his voice now.

"Of course they're going to care. They love you."

"No, but they're not going to disown me or something ridiculous, right? They're not that kind of parents. I keep telling myself they aren't, but what if they are?"

"Did they disown me?"

"No," he says, plopping down on the bed next to me.

"And I can control what I did. I did it of my own choosing. You didn't choose to be gay, and they know that. They're super liberal about pretty much everything."

"Except your tattoos."

"Well, yeah, but have you noticed Mom hasn't mentioned them once since I've been home? I think she's really growing as a person."

That gets a little smile out of him.

"I guess I'm also kind of worried that I'm getting all worked up about telling them and it's just going to be this little blip. Like no big deal, this is our son now. Thank you for sharing, Gideon." He says the last sentence in a pretty impressive impersonation of our mother.

"Obviously I have no clue how they're going to react. I can speculate with you all day long, but I know I'll never hit the nail on the head with them. They can be unpredictable, like every other person on earth."

He nods.

"But one time Dad told me that he wasn't so much disappointed in me for picking up and leaving the way I did as he was disappointed in the dreams he had for me. He was disappointed that he had been so narrow-minded when it came to what he wanted and expected of me."

"Really?"

"Yeah."

"God, they never stop shocking me."

"For real," I say. "I don't know that Mom sees it the same way, but that made me feel a lot better."

"They're pretty cool parents."

"Way better than the Cunninghams."

He stares at me blankly.

"You know, from *Happy Days*. The Fonz? 'Ayyy,' and all that stuff?"

"I know what you're talking about, I just don't know why you're referencing such outdated pop culture."

I shrug. "There was a marathon on one of those channels that no one ever remembers we get. Like channel 289. For future reference."

"Thanks for talking this through with me," he says.

"Yeah, no problem," I say. "And just think, if they disown you, you and I can strike off together somewhere and live off the land."

"You mean live off my bar mitzvah money."

"Well, yeah, something like that." I turn to leave.

"Wait, Ezra."

I look at him, and his face is so open and innocent somehow. It reminds me of when he was little and would get in trouble for something dumb like pouring cereal all over the floor.

"I don't want to pry and you don't have to tell me, but did you run out of money?"

I stare at him for a second. Someone finally asked.

"Yes."

He nods and chews his bottom lip.

"But it's okay. I'll figure it out. I'll get back to it eventually."

"That sucks and I'm sorry."

"Thanks, Gid."

Our mom yells up the stairs then to see if we're ready.

"Guess it's time to go," he says.

The drive to the restaurant is uneventful and our table's ready when we get there, so in no time we're seated and a basket of bread is placed in the middle.

I reach for a roll and know immediately I should have buttoned the top button of my shirt.

"Is that another tattoo, Ezra?" my mother asks, a little too loud. "How many do you have now?"

"Oh, come on, Ma," I say, buttering my roll. "I thought we've been over this. I thought you were okay with them."

"What mother would be okay with her child graffitiing their whole body like that? Where do you think you're going to be buried? No Jewish cemetery will take you."

"Pretty sure that's an old wives' tale, Ma," I say.

My father nods in agreement but doesn't offer an opinion. I swear he fears her wrath almost as much as Gideon and I do.

Gideon

I honestly was hoping that the Ezra tattoo conversation would take up the whole evening and then I wouldn't have to come out.

I can't seem to stop moving. Every time I try to control one part of my body, it's like the next part starts up. I go from tapping my foot, to bouncing my knee, to chewing my lip, to rapping my knuckles on my chair.

My dad tells me to stop, and I do, for a few minutes. But then the cycle starts all over again.

After we order, he turns to me. "What is going on with you, Gideon? You're like a whirling dervish over here."

I rub my palms together. They're slick with sweat.

"I know, I'm sorry." I take one look over at Ezra, and he smiles encouragingly. "There's just something I've been wanting to talk to you guys about."

"Okay," my mom says.

In the moment, I'm sure they think this is going to be about a college choice they won't approve of or maybe a plan for my senior year schedule that isn't optimal for my college applications.

"Well. It's just . . . It's that I'm gay."

I look from my dad, slightly stunned, to my mom, a little confused, to Ezra, who's giving me double thumbs-up like he's the Fonz.

My dad is the first to break the silence. "Is that what you've been so nervous about?"

"Well, yeah."

And then something completely bizarre and unexpected happens. My mother leaps up from the table and comes around to hug me. She squeezes my head and kisses my cheek.

"I am so happy for you, Gideon," she says, in between kisses. "I was getting so worried that you didn't show any interest in girls or anyone. I kept thinking you were going to end up alone."

"Ma," I say. "Ma." I can't stop smiling, I'm so relieved, but I'm pretty sure she's going to choke me to death.

"I know," she says without me even having to say anything else. She moves back around to her side of the table and sits down. She dabs at her eyes. "We're in public."

"So you're okay with this?" I ask.

"Of course," my dad says. "Why wouldn't we be?"

"Some people aren't," I say with a shrug.

"We're not that kind of people, Gideon," my mom says. "We want you to be healthy and happy and mostly just not to die alone."

Ezra rolls his eyes, but luckily she doesn't see.

"Thanks, Ma," I say.

"We should have a party."

"A what?"

"A party. My friend Cheryl had one for her son when he came out of the closet. It was a good time."

"How was Cheryl's son ever in the closet?" my dad asks, mostly looking at Ezra, who shrugs.

"I don't know about that," I say.

"We'll talk about it. We don't have to make any decisions tonight," she says.

"The other thing is . . ." I start to say as our food is delivered.

Everyone is distracted by their food for a few minutes, and my mother tsks when Ezra rolls up the sleeves of his shirt, exposing his other tattoos.

"You were about to say something else, weren't you, Gideon?" my dad says. "You might want to get it out now, before your mother starts nitpicking about your brother's tattoos again."

"Yeah, yes. Um, the other thing is that I'm kind of dating Kyle."

This news barely seems to faze them.

"That's so nice for you boys, honey," my mom says.

"Makes sense, you've always gotten along really well," my dad says.

I smile down at my chicken parmigiana and just hope that my mother was kidding about having a party.

seventeen

Kyle

On Thursday morning I have the big meeting about my "school problems," as my mom has been calling them. So instead of going to second period, I go down to the guidance office, where my parents are waiting for me along with Ms. Gupta, my guidance counselor, Mr. Nelson, and this other guy, "Call me Craig," who works for the school district to test kids with problems.

Ms. Gupta starts the meeting by describing my "problem areas" and then launches into the results from my testing. They all seem to agree I probably have dyslexia but not necessarily where I see letters backward, which is what everyone assumes dyslexia is like, just where it changes how I read and process things.

Apparently everything I've ever known about learning disabilities has been wrong. Because they don't actually make you stupid or unable to learn. They just put obstacles in your brain that make things harder.

It's still really complicated, but it doesn't actually feel like anything to be ashamed of.

My parents do most of the talking up to a certain point, but then people start talking about me like I'm not there. I try to pay better attention so I can speak on my own behalf, and that helps.

"How did he get so far in school without anyone catching it?" my mom asks. "I'm not pointing fingers at all. I should have been aware he was having trouble. I'm his mother. And I was aware, to a point. We started working harder at home to make sure he stayed caught up with his class. But I just thought he was kind of a flighty kid."

"He's gotten very good at compensating," Craig says. "He works hard at making up for his deficiencies by being organized. At least most of the time. But his writing is scattered and his comprehension just seems off for a kid who is obviously intelligent. I think his potential has been limited by the obstacles he has with reading."

I swallow and look away. It's hard to hear someone talk about you like that. Complimenting you in some ways, but talking about what's wrong with you in the next sentence.

I take a deep breath. "I also used to be in classes with my best friend, Gideon, like in elementary and middle school. It's not like he did my homework for me, but he would explain things to me the way I needed them to be explained. But now we don't have classes together like that. 'Cause he's basically AP everything."

"I have a feeling you learned some methods during those years for how to rethink and reorganize your brain, in part thanks to Gideon," Ms. Gupta says. "He's a nice kid, but I do want you to realize that you've done a lot of this on your own."

"I guess I don't understand how I have dyslexia when I don't have trouble with letters and stuff. Like, I know the whole Elvish alphabet."

"The Elvish alphabet," Call Me Craig says with a grin teasing his lips.

"Yeah, Gideon and I pass notes in Elvish."

I can feel my mom rolling her eyes, but then Mr. Nelson says something really awesome.

"You know, it's interesting," he says. "But I've read a lot about how much knowing a second language can help kids with dyslexia. It never said anything about the language having to be real."

"So this is just how it is for me?" I ask.

"Yes," Mr. Nelson says.

I hold back all the questions I have about next year and college and the rest of my life. Thinking about it makes my heart pound. I have enough to deal with at the moment.

By the end of the conversation it's decided that I need to take a couple of tests next week, and then there will be more meetings and further discussions and eventually maybe I'll know exactly what kind of learning disability I have.

Leaving the meeting, I somehow feel both better and worse.

Better because it wasn't as scary as I was expecting, but worse because soon enough everyone is going to know about me. Like, they'll have to tell my teachers and I'll have to tell my friends.

My day goes downhill from there.

Ruby's at the lunch table with her new boyfriend, Josh Barton, just as she had threatened last week. Of course this is the day that Gideon has a meeting during lunch, so it's not even like I can go sit with him and Sawyer and Maddie. I take the chair next to Buster after I go through the food line and zone out while stabbing at my school-issued meat loaf. The table buzzes around me, but I have plenty of things to think about.

For instance.

Josh Barton is a douche canoe of the highest order.

He's the kind of guy who wears his varsity jacket even when it's ninety degrees out. He always smells vaguely of wet dog and sweat. And he spits when he talks.

But for some reason he's the most popular guy in the senior class. I will never understand the high school hierarchy.

It makes sense that Ruby would be dating him now, seeing as how she's basically the most popular girl in the senior class. She was slumming with me for the past six months. It's a good thing she doesn't know I have a learning disability, or else she would realize how deep her slumming went.

I would hate to ruin her image with my issues.

I know I have no right to be jealous of her and Josh. And even though it's obvious that she and I aren't together any-more, there aren't any rumors swarming about our messy breakup, and from what I can tell, most people think it was mutual.

With ten minutes left in the period, I get up to throw my garbage out and decide not to go back to the table. It's just too much. I'd rather go wait for Gideon outside the student activity room and at least get to see him for a couple of minutes before we have to head to separate classes again.

I set off in that direction, feeling lighter.

Ruby

I wish I could let this go, this whole thing with Kyle, but it bugs the crap out of me. I follow him out of the cafeteria at a safe distance, telling Josh I need to get something from my locker and that I'll meet him in study hall in a few minutes.

Gideon comes out of the student activity room just as Kyle's about to open the door, and they do this goofy, awkward smiling thing at each other.

Neither of them has the balls to show much affection at school, which is probably a good thing, because I would want to wring their necks.

The bell rings and they part ways, never even noticing that I was right here, that's how up each other's asses they are. Gideon squeezes Kyle's arm before he walks away, and Kyle stands there making heart eyes at him as he leaves.

I decide to take my opening.

"Hey, Kyle," I say, approaching him from the side.

"Oh, hey, Ru."

How dare he call me Ru? I keep my anger off my face.

"I hope lunch wasn't too weird for you or whatever," I say innocently. "You seemed kind of upset."

"Um, well . . . It's weird. But I figure it'll be weird for you to see me and Gideon together, too. So no harm, no foul, right?"

"Right, just wanted to make sure," I say, continuing my innocent act. "You just had a look on your face that made me think you weren't doing so well."

He seems kind of surprised. "Oh. I had a . . . I had a . . ." He pauses, collecting his thoughts and looking at the spot where Gideon was standing moments ago. "It's nothing."

"Trouble in paradise already?" I ask, teasing him.

He rolls his eyes, finally seeing through me, I think. Thank God, I was starting to think he was a bigger idiot than I ever imagined.

"No, Ruby, everything is fine with Gideon. I was having a little trouble with one of my classes, but we're working it out."

"Seems like having trouble in school is something you'd talk to your girlfriend about," I say, my anger rising again.

"I did mention it to you, a couple weeks ago. About having to talk to Ms. Gupta?"

"Oh."

"I wasn't really ready to talk about the details. I'm still not."

"Are you failing?" I ask.

"Well, no. I mean . . . Kind of. I don't really want to talk about it."

I study him now, trying to figure out what half-truth he just told me. It's there and I'm sure I could pull the rest of it from him, but then the late bell rings.

"Ah, crap," he says. "I gotta go. See you, Ruby."

And like that, he's gone. But there's definitely something up with Kyle. Maybe I should make it my mission to find out. Because just think of it, I could have dirt on Kyle and dirt on Gideon and then . . .

I shake my head at myself.

And then nothing.

Who cares?

Graduation is less than two months away. Why am I even entertaining any thoughts about game playing?

If I hadn't left my phone at home this morning, I would delete Gideon's lists right this second. I make a mental note to do that later after school.

I turn down the next hallway and head off in the direction of my actual boyfriend.

He's not the brightest guy on earth, but he's definitely hot. Except for when he gets excited and spits when he talks. I'm trying to convince myself that it's an endearing quality.

It's not.

eighteen

Kyle

I ring Gideon's doorbell at seven on Saturday night.

I had this awful premonition that for the first time in the history of hopping the fence I'd end up ripping my favorite jeans in the process. Hence the front door instead of the back.

The door swings open and Ezra stands there. I'm pretty sure he's trying to be intimidating.

"I'm guessing you're here to see my little brother," he says. He's doing that thing guys do, where they cross their arms and flex and then use their fists to kind of prop up their biceps and make them look bigger.

"Um, yeah," I say, standing at my full height, which is a solid four or five inches taller than Ezra. I can be intimidating, too.

"What are your intentions?" he asks.

I raise my eyebrow. "Are you serious?"

"Where do you see yourself in five years?" he asks. And then he bursts out laughing before punching me in the arm. "I'm just playing with you."

He moves out of the way of the door and heads toward the stairs as Gideon comes racing down them.

"Just make sure you have him back by ten," Ezra calls from the top of the stairs.

"I'm really sorry about him," Gideon says, shaking his head.

"No worries," I say.

"I thought we were going to meet outside."

"Yeah, well, my mom kept looking at me and I was getting antsy," I explain.

"Yeah, my mom was doing the same thing until she got on the phone with my aunt Gail. Then it got a little worse, because I had to listen to her talk about me." He shoots an annoyed look toward the back of the house, where I can hear his mom's muffled voice and laughter.

"My mom offered to let me borrow her car," Gideon says, holding up a set of keys.

"Awesome. It'll be nice to drive in a car that doesn't smell like old coffee."

We get into his mom's car and sit for a second.

"Where are we going?" he asks.

"Oh, um . . . I guess we never did decide that, huh?"

"Nope."

"Are you hungry?"

"I didn't eat dinner," he says. "I was kind of nervous and I wasn't sure what we were doing and my mom made meat loaf and I wasn't in the mood."

I smile at his nervous babble. "I didn't eat either."

"I feel like we're supposed to do something different than we normally would?" he says, his voice holding a questioning note.

"I don't even know what we usually do, though," I say.

"Well, the last time we hung out just me and you, we watched Lord of the Rings."

"Yeah," I say, wiping my palms on my jeans.

"And you cried," Gideon says.

"And you tried to kiss me."

"I mean, I didn't really try. We just had a moment."

"Sure, sure, whatever you say."

"This time I'll try harder," he promises.

"Good, glad we got that out of the way."

"Where do people even go on dates? I've kind of, you know, never been on one." He looks so sad to admit it that I want to hug him. At least, that's what the new boyfriend in me wants to do. The longtime best friend kind of wants to tease him. But I hold back that impulse.

"Well, Ruby and I mostly hung out with you guys or baby-sat her brothers and sister. Or went to school stuff," I say.

"I guess I don't really know what dating looks like in terms of our friendship?" he says, the worry in his voice getting stronger.

"Listen," I say, taking his hand. "Just because we didn't

come up with some perfect first-date plan together doesn't mean we're a failed couple or anything."

"So you really do want to do this? With me?"

"Of course," I say.

He lets out a sigh and nods. "I don't know if this sounds like anything worthwhile, but I saw a flyer earlier saying that they're showing *The Lion King* in the park behind the pool tonight. They were going to show it at the community center, but since it's been so nice lately they made a last-minute change to outside."

"We could go pick up some food or something," I say.

"There's a blanket in the trunk."

"Maybe I should grab some sweatshirts from my car."

"Why do you have multiple sweatshirts in your car?"

"Because I never bother to bring them inside?"

"So you have multiple dirty sweatshirts in your car?"

"They might be of dubious cleanliness, but I figure if I just get them from my car, then neither of us have to face our mothers again."

"Fair point," Gideon says, rubbing his chin. "I would appreciate it if you found me one that doesn't smell too bad."

After sniffing through a pile of hoodies, I get back into Gideon's car and we set off in the direction of the sandwich place, where we each get an Italian sub, a bag of chips, and a cupcake.

When we get to the park, Gideon pauses by the car with a worried expression.

"What?" I ask.

He swallows heavily and nods toward the field up ahead. "I'm a little worried about what's going to happen when the people out there realize we're together on what's pretty obviously a date."

It's a valid concern. Neither of us have really ever been *out* in the way that people normally associate with "being out."

"We can do whatever makes you comfortable," I say, putting my hand on his arm. "We don't have to be really obvious or anything. We can just be two friends, hanging out on a blanket, sharing a sandwich, and watching *The Lion King*. Two bros on the town."

He sucks in a huge breath and then blows the air out slowly.

"And we don't have to do this. We could just go home. It doesn't matter."

He nods.

"But people around here are pretty accepting in general. Remember those two guys who were seniors when we were freshmen? They were out all the time, holding hands, putting their arms around each other. No one said a thing."

"They did get their gym clothes flushed down the toilet."

"That's true," I say. "Some soggy gym clothes are worth it to hang out with you."

"Kyle, that is a really beautiful and cheesy sentiment," he says, putting his hand on my shoulder. "But honestly, how can you be so sure about all this?"

"I don't know. I guess I figure one of us has to be. You'll pick up the slack somewhere else in the relationship. Isn't that kind of how it's always been with us?"

He swallows again and then stands up straighter, holding our food in one hand and the sweatshirt I loaned him in the other. I take the sweatshirt from him and bundle it in with the blanket and my jacket before taking his hand.

"Is this okay?" I ask, gesturing to our hands.

"Yeah, I think I need that."

We take a seat pretty far back from the screen. There are kids running around in front of the screen, back and forth between blankets from one family to another, obviously all playing some kind of game. We watch them while we eat our dinner because the movie doesn't start for another fifteen minutes, but they're just as entertaining.

No one pays any attention to us until one little kid, maybe four or five, runs across our blanket and trips.

Gideon leans forward quickly to help him up. "You okay?" he asks.

The kid looks at Gideon with wide eyes and then runs in the other direction.

"You're welcome!" Gideon calls after him.

I shake my head and try to suppress a laugh.

"Kids today have no manners," he says, turning to me.

"You're kind of adorable, you know?"

He blushes, so I lean over and kiss his cheek, hoping to make him blush even more.

When the movie starts, all the kids quiet down and give their attention to the animals up on the screen. I ball up the extra blanket I grabbed for us to use as a pillow. I lie back on it and then Gideon lays his head on my chest.

It feels just the way it's supposed to.

An older woman walks past us and says, "Aren't you two just adorable?"

Gideon hides his face in my chest and groans in embarrassment.

"I like this new side of you," I tell the top of his head. "This cuddly, bashful person who blushes at the drop of a hat."

"I'm just really happy," he says, rolling away from me and leaning up on his elbow. "I'm so happy it makes me want to hide, because I don't know what to do with it all. I want to store it up and save it for winter."

"But winter just ended."

"Fine, I want to store it up and save it for when I don't feel like it's bursting from every single one of my pores. I didn't know this was possible. To feel this way."

I lean up on my elbow to face him, smiling.

"What? Are you going to make fun of me?" Gideon asks.

Someone shushes us from a nearby blanket, so I pitch my voice low and whisper in his ear. "I can't make fun of you because I feel the exact same way."

We settle back down and watch the movie, falling silent for most of it as the story unfolds before us.

"I haven't seen this in a really long time," Gideon says at one point.

"I know. I feel like I forgot half the plot."

"And you miss so much when you're a kid. A lot of this went way over my head," Gideon says.

When the movie is over, we pick up our blankets and stumble to the car, half in a daze. Gideon parks the car in his driveway and then walks me to my door, our hands intertwined.

"So this was a real date?" he asks.

"I would say it was a very successful real date."

"Good, good. Maybe we should do it again sometime."

"I think I'm supposed to wait three days before calling you or something, though."

"Well, that's going to be a problem, because today is Saturday and on Monday I'm going to need a ride to school," Gideon says with a grin.

"Oh, right, yeah. There goes that idea."

"You're not cool enough to wait three days anyway. You want everything right away. Instant gratification."

"That's true," I admit.

"I really did have fun tonight," he says.

"Me too. I was kind of worried there for a second in the beginning that you were going to freak out and just want to go home."

"I'm way cooler than that," Gideon says. "Or at least now I am."

"See you tomorrow?"

"Yeah, see you tomorrow."

He leans in, kisses my cheek, and then jogs away.

Damn that was perfect.

nineteen

Ruby

There are less than two months left until graduation, and I finally have to come to terms with the fact that I might not have enough money to cover all my college costs in the fall. I'd still really like to live on campus. But if I don't get loans, there's no way that's happening with my parents' financial situation. Hopefully it's not too late to apply.

I scan the financial aid bulletin board in the guidance office, trying to figure out what would work for me without actually having to tell anyone what my problem is. I almost roll my eyes at how desperately I'm trying to keep control of my image. But it's just this one thing. I would like to leave high school mostly unscathed, without people feeling sorry for me or realizing just how poor I am.

I finally come to terms with the fact that I'm going to need to actually talk to a guidance counselor when Kyle appears from one of the offices. He's chewing his thumbnail, looking nervous and a little bit twitchy, like he doesn't want anyone to see him. Takes one to know one, I guess.

I try to hide a little, turning toward the ficus plant in the corner of the office. But I guess that little bit of movement is enough to call attention to me.

"Hey, Ruby," Kyle says.

"Oh, hey," I say. "What's up with you?"

"Um, well," he starts, and then glances behind him. "Just needed to have a meeting with people, about stuff."

"So you really are failing a class," I say.

"Kind of?" he says, squeezing one eye closed. "I was, but I'm probably not anymore because . . ."

At that moment his parents file out of the office behind him.

"Because you ran to Mommy and Daddy and they're taking care of everything?" I mutter. I can't help but be annoyed. I hate kids who do stuff like that. As if they can't take care of their own business. My parents would never come in to have a conference with my guidance counselor just to bail my ass out.

"No," he says, but doesn't have a chance to continue.

"Oh, hello there, Ruby," Mrs. Kaminsky says, coming up to me and giving me a hug right there in the guidance office.

"Ruby," Mr. Kaminsky says. I swear if the man were wearing a hat, he would have tipped it.

"Hi," I say, none too warmly. I always thought the Kaminskys were better than this. That they made their kids take responsibility for their shortcomings.

"How's everything going with college? Have you made your final decisions? I know you were getting close last time I saw you, but it's been a while," Mrs. Kaminsky asks.

She's too damn nice for her own good, I think, as I say and do the right things for the next ninety seconds. I make small talk and remind myself that Mrs. K in particular has never been anything but kind to me.

"Well, we'd better get going," Kyle's dad says.

"Yes," Mrs. K says, squeezing Kyle's arm. "We'll see you later, sweetie." Then, turning to me, "It was good to see you, Ruby. I'm glad to hear that things are going well."

I smile. It's a little tight-lipped, but I manage it.

When they leave I expect Kyle to follow them, but instead he turns back to me, his expression angry and put off.

"For the record, I didn't run to Mommy and Daddy about this. If anything, I didn't even want them involved."

"Yeah, right," I say, sort of shocked by how passionate he is. "You rich kids are all the same."

"Seriously?"

"I thought you were different. I thought maybe you had a little more self-respect."

He shakes his head. "You have no clue what's going on."

"I know what was going on. Gupta gave you a bad grade and you turned into a whiny little bitch." I'm not sure where this anger toward Kyle is coming from, but now that I started I can't seem to stop.

"I can't believe I'm telling you this. I shouldn't have to

defend myself to you, but as it turns out, I have a learning disability that no one ever noticed before."

That gets my attention. Before I can say anything, he continues. "Like, that's why reading has always been so hard for me. But now I had to take all these tests, and it turns out all this time being disorganized and having a hard time was mostly because of this thing. That I have no control over."

I stare at him. He looks like he might cry and then takes a deep breath and hitches his thumbs through the straps on his backpack.

"You're the only person who knows. So I would appreciate it if you didn't mention it to anyone." He stares at the bulletin board next to us, and his whole body radiates discomfort.

"No, of course not," I say. "I'm sorry. I'm sorry I assumed."

"Whatever."

Then he shrugs coolly and walks out.

I'm left standing there, trying to process all this new information.

Kyle

After talking to Ruby, I know I need to tell Gideon everything as soon as possible. The last thing I want is for someone besides me to tell Gideon my news. Ruby said she wouldn't say anything, but I'm not sure I can trust her.

I don't see him after school, and then I remember that he has a yearbook meeting. He's going to be editor next year, and he takes the whole thing so seriously. As he takes pretty much everything.

Because he's Gideon.

We hadn't made plans for after the meeting. He usually gets a ride home with Maddie, so it would be silly for me to wait, but today isn't a usual day.

I decide to go hang out outside and pull my car across the parking lot so I'm parked right next to hers. Then I hop up on the trunk and settle in to wait for Gideon.

It's a pretty nice day outside, so that helps.

I know I have plenty of things I should be doing at home. There is this whole new plan for how I'm going to tackle homework and assignments from now on. But it doesn't really seem as important as making sure I talk to Gideon.

I think I might have even dozed off for ten minutes when a voice next to me says, "Hey, I thought you'd be long gone by now." Gideon is standing next to my car with a huge smile on his face.

I sit up, feeling a little dizzy and out of sorts after lying in the same position for so long in the afternoon sun. "Um, yeah. It's just—" I start to say, and then I notice Maddie is still standing there.

"Hey, Maddie."

"Hey, Kyle. You look like you got some sunburn," she says.

I touch the tip of my nose, and it's really warm. "Oh man!"

"It's kind of cute," she says. "I promise."

"Hey!" Gideon says. "Stop flirting with my man."

She swats him with her bag and then opens her car door. "I'm assuming Kyle will give you a ride home."

I nod.

"Cool. See you guys tomorrow."

She drives off.

"So, really, what's up?" Gideon asks, turning back to me.

"I wanted to talk to you about something," I say, hopping off the trunk. "Wanna go hang out in the park?" I gesture toward the little plot of green that's across from the school. It's barely a park, but it has a Revolutionary War monument in it, so I guess it counts.

"Sure, but I'm not gonna lie, you're kind of freaking me out."

"No, it's nothing to worry about," I say. We both toss our bags in the car, and I take his hand as we cross over to the empty park.

"Just tell me right now," he says as we sit. "Are you breaking up with me?"

"No, Gideon, seriously, nothing like that."

I take a deep breath. "I'm a little nervous about this."

"You think you're nervous. I'm having heart palpitations."

At least that makes me smile, and I feel a little more normal. I bounce my knee up and down and Gideon puts a hand on it, stilling me, making me feel even better.

"So you know how I've kind of always had trouble reading?"

"I guess?" he says.

"Like, you wanted me to read the Lord of the Rings and *The Hobbit* and a million other books and I never did?"

"Yes."

"Well, I never make a big deal about it, but reading is just not fun for me. It's hard, and, like, I read too fast or too slow and the words never really make sense."

Gideon's looking at me with such concern that I know I need to speed up this explanation before he starts to assume I have brain cancer or something.

"The past couple weeks, I've been getting tested for learning disabilities. My parents came in and we had meetings. It all started with Ms. Gupta."

"Are you okay?"

"Yeah," I say. "I'm fine."

"But do you have one? A learning disability?"

"Well, yeah. It's basically dyslexia, but there are some other issues mixed in there that can go along with dyslexia, but they're not really sure. But that's why I have such trouble with reading comprehension. And organization. And even knowing my left from my right."

"You're dyslexic?"

"Yes. Like I said, there might be more to it than that, but that's what they're leaning toward."

"How did no one know this before? Like, how do you get through so many years of school without anyone noticing?"

"I mean, honestly, you used to help me with everything, all the time. We were always in the same class in elementary school and then mostly the same classes in middle school. It was only really in high school where we got split up. And I guess no one really noticed, because I know how to compensate. It wasn't until Ms. Gupta took over my English class that anyone really noticed."

"I helped you?" he asks.

"God yeah, all the time. Looking back, you helped me more than anyone else."

He's quiet then for a minute, and that minute stretches into two.

I feel like I might not be able to take it anymore when he finally speaks. "Why were you so nervous to tell me?"

I shrug. "I didn't want you to think I was stupid."

"I would never, ever think that about you," he says, shaking his head slowly and looking me in the eye. "You're so much more than just how you do in school. You're my best friend. You're my favorite person on earth."

"Thanks. You're all that stuff to me," I say.

Gideon lets out a long breath and I do the same.

"Thanks for telling me," he says.

"I didn't want it to turn into a fight like when I came out to Ruby, so I figured I'd tell you as soon as I knew the facts."

We walk back over to the school building, and I tell him all about the meeting where they decided that part of why I got so good at compensating was thanks to learning Elvish.

Gideon loves it.

He eats it right up.

twenty

Gideon

I'm in the hallway after physics class. I'm not thinking anything in particular, except that I don't want to go into the chemistry classroom until the teacher in there is done giving that other kid a talking-to. He doesn't look like he's having a good time.

It's Friday. I just want this week to end so I can spend time with Kyle, since he's still on lockdown on school nights.

Ruby and Josh come up the stairs from the opposite direction. She has her arm threaded through his and a big smile on her face.

I shrink in next to the wall, half hiding myself around the corner, because really the last thing I want to do is interact with my boyfriend's ex-girlfriend. And her big, stupid, mean jock of a new boyfriend.

Josh has never been a favorite person of mine. He's the kind of guy in gym class who picks out the weakest one in the herd. I'm not usually the weakest, but I'm usually second or third, so if those other guys are absent, I'm up shit creek. I have taken one too many dodgeballs in the chest.

Logically, I get it. I'm on the small side. Even if five-seven going on five-eight isn't really that short, some of the gorillas at this school seem to think it is. And I could still grow. I only just turned seventeen. Lots of guys grow even when they're in college.

But like it or not, I am a small guy right now. I can't change that, and for some reason guys like Josh Barton take that personally, so they spike volleyballs at my head in the name of physical education.

I've spent a solid chunk of my high school career avoiding him and his ilk. Hence my involuntary response to seeing him is to shrink. Become one with the wall.

Luckily, he doesn't see me. He seems to be listening to Ruby. I can't hear what she's saying from here, but I don't think Josh is particularly impressed. His gorilla face seems kind of angry. And then it goes from angry to enraged.

"For Christ's sake, Ruby, I am so tired of hearing about this. All you do is talk shit about people. I don't care what those cheerleader chicks are doing. I just really don't, and I don't know why you think I do."

"Fine. I'll stop talking about it," she says. She shrugs and backs away from him a little, like she's scared he might get violent. If I were a better person, I would make myself known, because it's kind of obvious that his anger made her nervous. "No big deal."

"Nah. You know what? I'm done," he says, shaking his head. "I think we should break up. You're not as much fun as everyone made you out to sound."

"But—" she says.

He cuts her off. "No. I think you got way too into that pansy Kaminsky, and now you don't even know how to be a decent girlfriend anymore."

The second he drags Kyle's name into this I want to leap out from my hiding spot and scream and yell and claw his eyes out. But I'm probably just as weak as guys like Josh Barton think I am, because instead I stay frozen, barely breathing.

"Well, that's a crappy thing to say," Ruby says. "And Kyle's not a pansy."

"I see him all over the place, him and his pansy-ass boy-friend."

"Stop saying that, stop calling them that."

"Pansy, pansy, pansy."

I peek around the corner just as Josh slips into the boys' room.

"We're done," he says, backing through the door, dramatically wiping his palms together, like he's dusting Ruby off them.

Ruby slumps against the lockers across from the doorway and slides down. On the way, her bag snares on the lock and rips open at the seam.

"Shit," she says. "Shit, shit, shit."

Their whole conversation happened within thirty seconds, and just as I'm wondering why we're still the only people in this hallway, I hear the tide of other students coming in our direction. I look again to where Ruby is scrambling to pick up all her belongings and decide to be a good guy.

"Hey," I say, kneeling down to grab for loose pieces of paper and some gum wrappers that are strewn about. "That sucked."

Ruby's crying, but I pretend not to notice. "You heard what he said?"

"Yeah, I was over there," I say, pointing vaguely over my shoulder. "I didn't mean to listen, I swear."

She rolls her eyes at me. "Of course you're the one who saw what happened. Of course." She swipes at her eyes with her fingertips.

"I'm sorry," I say. And I mean it. I'm sorry about everything that happened. It all sucks, but I don't have a chance to say anything else because she grabs her stuff from me and hugs it close to her chest before making a break for it down the hall and out of sight.

Kyle

I come up behind Gideon at his locker after school and poke him in the side.

"Oh God, iron finger," he says, bending over a little. "Why do you have the pointiest fingers on earth?"

"It's a mystery."

"Did you hear about Ruby and Josh?" he asks, pitching his voice low.

"I heard they broke up."

"They exploded. I was standing there the whole time they were fighting, and it was a complete horror show."

He goes on to fill me in on all the gory details about how it went down. He pauses halfway through and takes a deep breath, like a doctor about to deliver bad news. "Josh called you a pansy, and I feel like such a coward for not walking up to him and knocking his teeth out."

I squeeze Gideon's shoulder, trying to comfort him even though it makes me feel slightly sick to my stomach.

"It happens," I say.

"A good boyfriend would have totally defended your honor and knocked his teeth out."

"Yeah, but then that boyfriend would have been suspended from school and it would have tarnished his record."

"Good point," he says. "But then he called me a pansy, too. Ruby was kind of, sort of trying to defend us, but she was so clearly upset at that point."

I try not to think about how much better it makes me feel to know that Josh called both of us pansies.

"At least we're pansies together," I say, making a joke of it.

He smiles. "Anyway, the worst part was after Josh walked away, Ruby's bag got caught on a locker and the seam basically exploded."

"Oh man. Insult to injury."

"Exactly. So I went over to help, but she wasn't exactly in a good place. I just feel bad that it had to happen at all. I'm left feeling, well, the best word for it is icky. There's no good word for it. I just feel completely icky," Gideon says.

"That sucks." I try to think of something to lighten the mood. "So are you planning on breaking up with me now, too? Seeing as how we've basically been together about the same amount of time? Aren't breakups supposed to happen in threes?"

"I thought that was deaths, but sure, let's go with it."

"Fine, bad things happen in threes," I say.

"I mean, it's only been two weeks. I think I should give you a little bit more of a chance. I'm not a quitter," Gideon says, puffing his chest out.

"It's, like, just barely a week since we went on our first date," I tell him.

For once Gideon doesn't check every nook and cranny of the entire school before kissing me on the cheek. It's just a little peck, but it feels like a big move forward, considering everything that Gideon witnessed earlier and how nervous he usually is about public displays of affection.

"I like that you know that," he says.

We turn around and head down the hall, holding hands in the nearly empty school.

"What are we doing today?" I ask.

"Whatever you want. Do you need help with anything?"

I pause as we're about to go through the heavy front doors and pull his hand to stop him.

"I don't. They're still coming up with a plan for me, and Ms. Gupta is helping me with my English paper. But thanks for asking."

"Thanks for not being offended that I asked," he says.

Ruby

Kyle and Gideon don't even notice Lilah, Lauren, and me around the corner in the senior hallway as they walk out of the building. But we definitely notice them.

"God, they're so gross," Lilah says.

"You can't call gay people gross," Lauren tells her. "It's, like, against the law. It's a hate crime."

"I'm not saying they're gross because they're gay. I'm saying they're gross because they're all, like, lovey-dovey and flaunting it."

"But did you say it because they were gay? Do you think other couples are gross?"

"I think any couple that I'm not a part of is completely gross," Lilah says.

Lauren nods sympathetically. "What do you think, Ruby?" she asks.

"I think I hate everyone. I can't believe I messed everything up with Josh, and Gideon was there to see the whole thing go down. I don't even know how that happened. Like, why was he the one person who had to be there to see everything fall apart?" I slide down the locker and land on the floor. At least this time my bag doesn't get caught and fall apart. Oh, that's right, that's because that already happened today, so I don't have a bag anymore.

"So what are you going to do?" Lilah asks, sitting next to me on the floor.

"Yeah, we should plot revenge," Lauren says, sitting next to her.

I pick up my phone to check the time. I need to be at Marco's baseball practice at four thirty to pick him up, but we still have about a half hour until I have to leave.

"The first thing I need to do is change the lock screen on my phone," I say, when I notice it's a picture of Josh and me. I unlock the phone and go into my pictures, but Lilah pulls the phone out of my hand.

"Oh my God," she says, scrolling through my albums. "You have to delete so many pictures. Good-bye, Josh, good-bye, Josh."

I smile. Her dramatics are at least entertaining.

"Why do you still have pictures of Kyle?" she asks, turning to show me one of him and me hanging out at the diner a couple of months ago.

Lilah hits the little trash can to delete it.

"Good-bye, Kyle," Lilah says, waving at the screen, and then deletes another and another. Then she stops and tips her chin down, zooming in on something. "What is this? Is this a list?"

Lauren leans over. "A list of everything that's wrong with Kyle Kaminsky."

"Does it say 'tiny penis'? 'Cause I'm pretty sure it should say that."

"Shit, delete that," I say. I meant to get rid of it and the other ones so many times, but they were so far back in my pictures that I just kept forgetting.

"Hell no," Lilah says. "Who wrote this?"

"Not me," I tell her.

"OMG, was it Gideon? Did Gideon write this?"

"It's a long story." I try to grab for the phone but Lilah pulls away from me, tapping at the buttons and making me nervous.

"Perfect boyfriend Gideon, talking shit and writing mean lists," Lauren says, shaking her head.

"Just delete it. Come on, guys. I don't want to mess around with this stuff. It's not worth it. I'm trying to be mature."

"You don't have to be mature," Lauren says.

"Or you can be and I'll take care of this for you," Lilah says.

"Lilah, what are you doing?"

Her phone vibrates in her bag.

"Nothing," she says innocently.

She hands me back the phone and the list is gone, but I have a bad feeling she sent it to herself.

"What are you going to do?" I ask again.

"Nothing. It's just a little insurance. I don't want anyone to make my friend feel bad."

"Delete it from your phone," I say slowly, hoping she understands from my tone that I'm not fooling around anymore.

"Fine, fine," she says after one more second where I feel like my heart is in my throat. "You can even do it yourself."

She hands me the phone, and I delete the text she sent herself and her most recent photos just to be on the safe side. I'm sure there are other places she could have hidden it, but honestly, I don't think she's that smart.

"Happy now?" she asks.

"Yes, very."

"Good. Let's go find something to do to cheer you up." She and Lauren stand and put their hands out for me, pulling me up off the floor.

Because that's what friends do. They pull you up when you need them to.

twenty-one

Gideon

On Saturday I spend the day volunteering for Habitat for Humanity. I've tried to get Kyle to come with me for years, but he just refuses, and this time was no different. He told me he needed to play video games with Buster.

At least I can always trust him to be honest with me.

When we turn onto my street, it's almost eight o'clock, because I spent the last couple of hours eating pizza with Maddie and Sawyer and a bunch of other people from the crew. I like being part of a "crew."

"Dude," Sawyer says. "There are a lot of people at your house right now."

"Oh crap," I say. "I'm pretty sure my mom mentioned this to me and I completely ignored her."

"What did she tell you?" Maddie asks.

"Something, something, Saturday night. Party. Home by seven?" I check my phone, and sure enough, about forty-five minutes ago I got a "Where are you?" text from my mother, followed by a "You better get your ass home soon" text from Ezra.

"Freaking awesome," I say. "Any chance you guys want to come in and create a diversion so I can get up to my room and shower?"

Sawyer sniffs his armpit and shakes his head as Maddie says, "Definitely not."

They drop me off a few houses away, because there's literally no place to pull over and our driveway is overflowing. When I walk up to the house, I can see Ezra sitting on the front porch, wearing his version of "dress-up clothes": a blue button-down shirt rolled up at the elbows that I'm sure our mom threw a fit over and a pair of navy slacks that he probably borrowed from our dad.

I get to the top step and look over at him in the glow from the porch light. He's sitting in one of the rocking chairs that no one ever sits in.

"Please tell me one thing," I say.

He nods.

"Is she really having a coming-out party for me?"

He laughs so hard he almost rocks the chair backward off the ground.

"You'll just have to go inside and find out, won't you?"

"I don't think I'm ready for this."

Ezra gets up and hooks a brotherly arm around my neck. "You were born ready."

We go into the house and my mother's standing there in a cocktail dress and pearls, a little overdressed compared to everyone else in the house, I notice.

"Ma, I thought you were joking about the coming-out party!" I say to her.

"I was mostly. This is actually a party for someone in Daddy's office who's retiring, but it seemed like a good time for you to tell everyone your good news, too."

"How many people have you told?" I ask.

"Oh, not that many." She looks around as if counting heads, and that makes me nervous. Then she kisses my cheek.

"It's not really your news to tell, you know that, right?"

"I know that, Gideon. I promise I didn't tell anyone you wouldn't have. Now go upstairs and shower before anyone else gets a whiff of how awful you smell."

I roll my eyes but follow her instructions obediently, mostly because I hate being dirty. And if I can smell myself, I can only imagine how bad I must smell to other people.

Before I shower, I take another glance at my cell phone, hoping to hear from Kyle. Maybe he'll get home early from Buster's and decide he wants to come hang out over here for a little while. Sadly, I have zero texts.

After a quick shower, I get out, try to tame my hair, put on some "decent" clothes, and head back downstairs to the party.

Ezra spends most of the next hour following me around and forcing me to talk to people from my father's work about my new "lifestyle choice." I make sure to elbow him in the kidney every time he says something inappropriate. By the end of the night I'm sure he'll have a pretty decent bruise. But the man is unstoppable. He just loves making a spectacle of himself.

He finally decides to sneak me a tall glass of Coke with the lightest splash of rum in it and then acts like I should be forever grateful.

"You're underage. You're lucky I gave you anything at all. I could go to prison."

"I'm pretty sure you can't go to prison for giving a seventeen-year-old the barest vapors of rum. I don't think that's how the justice system works."

We wander around the room, being the good little sons our parents expect us to be. Several people congratulate me; mostly they just ask what my college plans look like. Now that's something I don't mind talking about at all.

I have no idea how much time has passed, but at one point one of the partners' wives pulls me aside and basically wants to gossip. She asks a lot of questions about how school is going. Apparently she has a daughter who is a freshman, but I don't know her.

"So are you dating anyone? Because I also have a son who's in his second year at Drew who might be interested."

"I am in fact dating someone," I tell her, trying to look at least somewhat sorry to reject her son.

I excuse myself and decide that I've waited long enough to look at my phone. My parents are stuck in a loop of conversation with some old man in the corner. I can tell by the sad looks in their eyes that they don't know how to get out of it.

My mother tries to pull me over with her death stare, but I make a beeline for the stairs and head for the peace and quiet of my room.

At least for a few minutes.

Kyle

Spending the day playing video games with Buster was both a wonderful and terrible decision. We lose all track of time. We probably would have never left the cocoon of his room if it wasn't for hunger.

Around seven o'clock he calls for a pizza, forcing him to look at his phone for the first time in hours. He pauses the game and unlocks his phone.

"Dude," he says, making a face at the screen.

"What's up?" I ask.

"Do you have any texts?"

I root around in the couch cushions for my own phone, having felt it slip out when it was still light out. I grab it and unlock it, but I've got nothing. I'm a little sad that I haven't heard from Gideon, but I'm pretty sure he's probably still busy with his volunteering thing.

"There's, like, this text," Buster says, staring at his phone.

"Okay."

"A list."

"Come on, Buster, use your words and explain what's going on."

He gives me the finger and then he opens and closes his mouth a few times before just handing me his phone.

And it is a text, with a picture of a list. The text says "Pass it on," and the list is written in neat penmanship on binder paper.

I zoom in. It's Gideon's handwriting. I would know it anywhere.

The title of the list is "Everything That's Wrong with Kyle." The first thing on the list is *He's too tall*. I almost start to laugh, because it's gotta be some kind of joke. I mean, obviously I'm tall. But is there really such a thing as *too tall*? Does Gideon really think that of me?

My throat tightens as I continue reading. *He's really awkward sometimes.* I lick my lips and try to swallow. I skim a bit more. Then I get to one that says, *He's not as smart as me.* That one hurts. That hurts a lot. But not as much as the one after it. *When I gave him the Lord of the Rings trilogy to read, he said he just "couldn't get into it." I even tried to get him to read* The Hobbit *and he wouldn't. And that's practically a kids' book.*

I toss the phone away like it's hot and try to understand what I was just reading. Buster looks at me like he's a dog that just had an accident on a new carpet.

"Dude," he says.

I rub my eyes with the heels of my hands until I see spots and that weird kaleidoscope of colors that usually makes me feel better. But it doesn't help.

"Are you okay?"

I shake my head. I definitely am not. I am really, really not okay.

"Did, uh, do you think, um, did Gideon write that?"

I look over at him and nod. "Who sent it to you?" I ask.

"Looks like some chick from my Spanish class. I wonder how long it's been going around," he says, tapping at his phone.

"Is it in a group text?" I ask.

"Yeah, a bunch of numbers, but I don't know any of them." He scrolls.

My hands are shaking, but I don't even know what I'm feeling. It's all one big blur of anger, shame, embarrassment, sadness. How could Gideon do this to me? After I told him everything that's been going on lately. He writes a list and takes a picture and just texts it out to people?

I must say this out loud because Buster answers. "It's not from Gideon, though."

"I know. But the 'pass it on' thing, it had to start somewhere."

"Yeah" is all Buster says. He's obviously not going to be much help here.

"I gotta go," I tell him.

"Yeah, I get it. See you, bro."

He walks me downstairs, looking at me like he's worried I might try to dive out a window or something.

"You gonna be okay?"

I shrug. I don't say what I'm thinking, which is that I probably won't be okay. This is all very not okay. "Can you text me that list?"

"Sure, if you really want me to." He looks at his phone and sends it.

"Thanks, man."

I head to my car and barely close the door before I start to cry.

Ezra

I'm talking to one of the young wives, flirting pretty obviously, pretending I'm on *Mad Men* or some shit, when Kyle comes bursting through the back door.

And believe me, it's pretty hard to burst through a sliding door. But somehow he manages it.

His nose is all red and his eyes are kind of glassy. Something is very wrong.

"Where's Gideon?"

"I think up in his room. He was going to find his phone because he missed you."

Kyle rolls his eyes.

"What's . . ." He gestures toward the front of the house.

"Parental cocktail party." I gesture at his face. "What's, uh, happening here?"

"Nothing good," he mutters. Then he moves fast down the hallway, threading between bodies and racing for the stairs, as much as you can race in a crowd.

Something is definitely wrong.

twenty-two

Kyle

I didn't realize there was a party going on at the Berkos'. That's how angry I was and still am. I made it all the way down the street and into their house without noticing the millions of cars everywhere, without seeing that all the lights were on downstairs.

After Ezra tells me where Gideon is, I weave my way through the party and up the stairs. I take a deep breath at the door to his room. It's half open, but my manners get the better of me and I knock on it once.

"Gideon," I call through the door.

"Hey," he says, pulling it open. "I was just about to text you." He smiles like he didn't do anything wrong. Like he didn't write a list of everything that sucks about me.

Like that list isn't completely true.

But that's not the point. Neither your best friend nor your boyfriend should ever make a list about you like that. It's not how it's supposed to be.

I step into his room and close the door behind me.

"We need to talk," I say, barely containing my rage, trying to keep my voice low so I don't disturb the party downstairs.

His face is confused and my hands flex involuntarily, like they want to touch him, but I can't. I can't let myself. He doesn't deserve anything from me.

"What's up?"

"What do you know about this?" I ask, pulling my phone out of my pocket and showing him the picture.

"Oh my God," he says. "What is this? Where did you get this?"

"I'm pretty sure you know what it is. Considering you wrote it."

To his credit, he looks sick to his stomach.

"Where did it come from?" he asks, looking up at me. His face is pale.

"Someone sent it to Buster." I grab the phone from him. "So you're not going to deny writing it or anything?"

"This isn't what you think it is. It's not what it looks like. I didn't—"

"Except you did," I say, interrupting.

"I didn't write it for anyone else to see. I wrote it when I'd just realized I liked you and I was trying to talk myself out of it."

"By being nasty? By saying mean things about me?"

"I'm not saying it was the best idea."

"You can't even just admit that this was shitty."

"It's out of context. There was more to it. It wasn't just about me trying to belittle you. You don't understand."

"Of course I don't understand. I'm bad at reading and I'm not as smart as you."

He stands up, as if he only now realized that we're having a fight and he's not going to take it sitting down.

"That's not at all what I said, and you know it."

"It's not what you said? Maybe I should read to you from the list. To refresh your memory." I pull my phone back out and read aloud. "'Everything that's wrong with Kyle. Number one, he's too tall.'"

Gideon tries to grab the phone from me, but I hold it up high and he would have to jump to even attempt to reach it. He's far too composed to ever do something that ridiculous.

"Hmm, guess I am too tall."

To my shock, Gideon does try to jump up and grab it, going so far as to stand on his bed and make a leap for it.

"Just delete it and let me explain," he says.

"No. I'm going to keep it forever so that if I start to mistakenly think you're an okay person, I can take it out and reread it. And you know, anytime I'm feeling really good about myself, I'll take it out and make sure I know that I suck. That I'm awkward and stupid and have a limited vocabulary and play too many video games."

"I really didn't mean any of that," he says, his voice cracking. "Let me show you the other things I wrote. That's just one thing. I was feeling so terrible and I didn't want to like you. I wanted to be friends with you and not ruin everything."

"Oh well, sure, the best way to do that is to write a really mean list. I totally understand now. It must have been my stupidity getting in the way."

"It's not what you think," he says.

"Maybe I should make a list about you. Gideon is short and too smart for his own good and walks like he has a stick up his ass."

He crosses his arms. "That's all completely fair."

I wish I could come up with more mean things to say about him, but of course in the moment my mind goes completely blank. Probably because I'm stupid, so instead I go back to his list.

"Just explain one thing to me: Who texted it?"

"I don't know. I guess Ruby."

"Ruby? How did Ruby know about it?" I can't shake the picture of Gideon and Ruby hanging out together, talking about me and laughing about how dumb I am.

"She was here one day, when we were playing Grand Theft Auto, and she found the binder where I made all these lists about liking you and not liking you and figuring out whether I was gay or whatever. She took pictures of them. I wasn't even out yet, but then she texted me a picture of one of the lists and kind of held it over my head."

"And now after all this time she just decides to text this one, terrible list?"

"I don't know. I'm not a mind reader. I thought she deleted the pictures."

There's a knock on the door.

"Boys?" Mrs. Berko says. "Are you okay in there? You're getting a little noisy."

Gideon opens the door. "We're in the middle of something, Ma."

"Well, we're in the middle of something downstairs, so maybe you guys could stop yelling."

"We'll be quieter," Gideon says.

"Actually, you don't have to worry about it, Mrs. Berko. I'm leaving."

"I'm sorry I didn't get to speak with you, Kyle," she says. "I feel like I barely see you now that you boys are together."

When she smiles, she looks so much like Gideon it pinches somewhere in my chest. I can't believe how messed up everything is.

I smile back, even though I'm sure it looks fake.

"I really should get going," I say.

"Wait," Gideon says.

I turn back and shake my head. "There's nothing else to say."

I leave Gideon looking stunned and his mother staring at him. I bolt down the stairs and out the front door without looking back.

There's nothing else for me there.

I never expected Gideon to be the one who would ruin it.

Gideon

I guess nightmares can come true.

But I never even had a nightmare about this. I never for one second thought anyone else would ever see that list about Kyle. And yet, here we are.

My mom just stands there looking at me. "Are you okay?" she asks.

"We had a fight," I say.

"Yes. I can see that."

"I'm sorry we disturbed the party."

She puts a hand on my shoulder. "You weren't really that loud. I just got worried because I could tell Kyle was upset and then I could hear your voices getting angry. It was a mother's intuition."

"I really messed up."

"I'm sure you can fix it."

"You don't have to stay here. You can go back to the party."

"Not if you need to talk," she says.

I take a deep breath. "Actually, what I really need to do is find this binder, but I'll let you know if I need to talk."

"You got it," she says. Then she pulls me in for a tight Mom hug, and for a second I just let myself be squeezed.

When she leaves, I dive under my bed, searching for my secret hiding place. When I open the Monopoly box, it's gone. But I could have sworn that's the last place I put it.

I start tearing my room apart. Maybe I moved it while I was sleepwalking or something. I have to find that binder and show it to Kyle in context. There's so much more to it than just that list.

Then I remember that the list doesn't even exist anymore.

I need him to listen to me, so I can explain. But I can't explain unless I find the binder.

I think about all my "safe" hiding places.

While I do that, I attempt to justify the list to myself. I was in such a bad mood that night, and I wanted to forget about liking Kyle. It seems so fruitless and unrealistic. It's a terrible list. It's malicious and nasty and not like anything I actually feel.

But it sucks that he saw it, because everything on that list is true. He knows it. And the truth hurts. Everything he said about me is true, too. I know he was just lashing out, but I almost wish he had said more. I deserve it after everything he saw on that list. Maybe if he ever speaks to me again, I'll tell him to make a list about me. Maybe that will make us even.

I look under my bed and through all my school stuff. I check the back of my closet with all my extra binders, in case I decided to put it away. I go through my desk and my dresser, and then I check the same places over again.

It's nowhere to be found.

It's after midnight when I slump on my bed and look at the clock. I have a bunch of texts from other people, asking me if I've seen the list going around about Kyle and was I really the one who wrote it. Maddie seems particularly angry about the whole thing. Probably because she has such a soft spot for Kyle.

I know the party has died down. The only noises from downstairs are the clatter and shuffle of my parents cleaning up. I should go help them, but I feel so exhausted.

I lie down on my bed fully clothed and fall into a fitful sleep.

twenty-three

Ruby

I think I need new friends.

This whole thing with Gideon and Kyle is all over school on Monday, and everyone is either super pissed or, worse, really happy about it. I can't handle any of it. I just want to go hide under a rock.

I spend most of the day avoiding Lilah and Lauren. I told Lilah to delete the pictures. It wasn't any of our business.

But the worst feeling is knowing that I should have deleted them myself a long time ago. I shouldn't have ever taken the pictures to begin with. I hate being the kind of person who wants to have something in her back pocket to use against someone else. When did I become that person? I don't like her.

I need to make this right.

People are seriously dragging Gideon through the mud. I don't know how he even had the nerve to show up at school today. Kyle didn't bother coming, but there's Gideon, trudging through the halls, trying to stay out of everyone's way. He's doing a pretty decent job, but every once in a while you'll see a group of people just stop in the middle of the hallway and talk about him. Pointing and whispering, not bothering to be a little bit subtle about it.

Gideon's a social pariah and I legit feel bad for him. Even Maddie and Sawyer don't seem to be talking to him. It's entirely my fault. I don't want to be the kind of person who puts the blame on other people. I don't want to be like that anymore. That's what I've been doing for months.

I've been telling myself the same sad story that my life sucks because my dad lost his job and because Kyle broke up with me and because Josh was mean. No, my life sucks because life sucks sometimes. I need to take responsibility for myself and my own happiness. And step number one is talking to Gideon and getting this all out in the open.

During lunch I make it my mission to track down Gideon. It's not like I want to go sit with those assholes I call my friends anyway. Better to find Gideon and try to make peace with him.

After looking all over the place, I find him in the student activity office. He's not even doing anything. He's just sitting there with his head in his hands. It's basically the worst thing I've ever seen.

"Feel free to rip my face off," I say. My voice startles him.

"I'm not going to rip your face off," he says. He's sad in a way that I've never seen anyone be sad. Gideon has always been the kind of guy who squares his shoulders and does what he needs to do. But today he looks so defeated.

"Well, do something to me, because I feel like complete crap about the whole thing," I say, taking a seat next to him.

"It's just as much my fault as it is yours," he says.

"And Lilah's, since she's the one who sent the text." I groan. "No, forget I said that. I literally just gave myself a stern talking-to about how I need to take responsibility for my actions, and then I come in here blaming Lilah."

"Lilah sent the text?"

"Yeah, but I never deleted the lists from my phone. Even though I obviously should have. And then she found them on Friday. I probably should have done more, but I was so upset about Josh."

"That thing with Josh was kind of terrible," Gideon says.

"I'm sorry I was a bitch to you in the hallway."

"Whatever, you were just lashing out."

"And then I made everything worse."

"It's over. It doesn't matter," he says.

"Of course it matters." I put my hand on his, and he looks surprised.

"I sent Kyle like eight hundred texts yesterday, and he ignored every single one of them. He probably blocked my number."

He looks so sad that I don't even know what to do, so I decide to tell him everything.

"All right, listen. I'm gonna come clean with you. I was so

sad that day at your house. And so jealous of everything you have. And then I went home and I found out my dad lost his job. You already had Kyle for a best friend, and I was so jealous of the thought of you also getting him as a boyfriend. Because I knew he would choose you over me. I just knew it."

"I didn't know it. I wasn't trying to steal him from you."

"I get that now. But back then it just seemed like you were going to end up with everything. And I was going to end up sharing a room with my sister for the rest of my life while I went to community college and worked full-time at Walgreens."

"I'm sorry. That sucks."

We're both quiet for a few minutes.

"There's no way I'm ever going to make this up to him," he says.

"Of course you will."

"How?"

"Where's the binder, Gideon?"

"I don't know," he says. "For a second I thought you had it."

"You thought I stole it?" I'm shocked. I've done some crappy things, but I definitely wouldn't have stolen his binder.

"Not stole it, but just kept it or something. I realize now that you didn't have anything to do with this." He shakes his head.

"So, then where is it?"

"It's missing. I put it under my bed in a box and it's gone."

"We need to find it. Because believe me, it was very convincing and showed me just how much you liked him. Even without being able to read Elvish, I was ready to fight for him. So maybe, if he reads it, he'll understand."

"You're gonna help me?"

"Hell yes."

When the bell rings signaling the end of lunch, I decide that maybe it's time for me to cut class. It's not something I've ever actually done before, but it feels like the right day. Maybe I can go talk to Kyle.

Or maybe there's someone else who might be able to help out.

Ezra

I should probably get a job.

Or maybe go to college.

I should probably work on a pro/con list and try to figure this out. I sit down at the kitchen table with a notebook and a pencil at the same second my phone dings with a text from an unknown number.

"Hey, Ezra. I need your help," it says.

"New phone. Who dis?" I write back.

"It's Ruby. Kyle and Gideon had a terrible argument and it's at least partially my fault and I was hoping you might be willing to help me get them back together."

"I had a feeling something bad was going down. Gideon spent all day yesterday in his room."

"Yeah, it's not good."

"What do you need me to do?" I type back.

"Well, first of all, there's this binder that Gideon had, and it's all full of lists that he wrote about Kyle."

"Gideon's 'I love Kyle' binder? I have it. I hid it. I had a feeling he couldn't be trusted with it. He kept hiding it in obvious places. First under the couch, then in a Monopoly box under his bed. Bad idea."

"I'm on my way over," she writes back.

Five minutes later the doorbell rings.

"Hey," I say, opening the door. "Shouldn't you be in school?"

"Technically yes, but I'm hoping since I'm a senior and I'm graduating in a couple weeks, no one will notice I'm gone. Just this once."

"Someone will notice. I mean, I would totally notice," I say. It's been a while since I did any kind of real flirting. I'm obviously rusty.

She smiles and punches me lightly on the shoulder.

"So, where's this binder?" she asks.

I lead her back through the hallway and out to the garage.

"I'd seen the binder around a couple of times, including the night I came home."

"Did you read it?" Ruby asks.

"Not so much. There was some stuff in Elvish and I was out of practice."

"You're all gigantic nerds," she says.

I shrug. She's not wrong. "Anyway, I haven't had much of a social life since I got home, so I was actually sitting down to play a rousing game of Monopoly with my parents several weeks back, so I went searching for it under Gideon's bed because he tends to hoard all the board games. Lo and behold, there was his secret binder. So I put it in an actual safe place."

I pull out the Rubbermaid bin where our mom stores our baby blankets and dig out the binder. I'm about to hand it to her, and then I pull back. "Why do you want this?"

"I want to show it to Kyle."

"Yeah, no. That sounds wrong." I hug the notebook to my chest as if I can protect it and Gideon at the same time.

"I took pictures of all the lists, and one of my friends found the one where Gideon lists all the things he doesn't like about Kyle and she texted it to everyone in her phone and it got around to basically everyone at school. I'm hoping that if Kyle sees the rest of the lists, he'll understand that Gideon likes him a lot, probably even loves him. And that one list was just a way for Gideon to try to talk himself out of Kyle."

"Does Gideon know about this?"

"Yes. It's totally Gideon sanctioned. He doesn't know that you had the binder this whole time, but he wants Kyle to see the other stuff in it."

I hand it to her. "All right. Fair enough."

She gets out her phone and starts texting. "I need to show it to Kyle right away. He didn't even come to school today."

"Why are you so invested in this?" I ask.

She shrugs. "I'm trying to right my wrongs, be a better person, all that good shit." Her phone buzzes. "Cool, he says to come over."

I follow her to the front door.

"So, listen. I don't know if you'd be into this, but maybe you want to hang out sometime?" I ask. "I'm getting a little tired of Monopoly with my parents."

She raises an eyebrow. "Maybe," she says. "You have my number."

And then she's gone.

It's definitely time for me to get on with my life.

twenty-four

Kyle

Everything is literally the worst. I lied to my mom about having a headache to get out of going to school today. I just couldn't face the people at school. Any of them. Not Gideon, not my friends, not Ruby. Everyone knows. The only good thing is that back when Gideon wrote the list, he didn't know what was wrong with me, so it's not like the whole school knows about my LD. But still. It feels like they do.

Oh God, and now Ruby's texting me. Is this just going to be her rubbing it in that I made the wrong choice? I don't even really want to look. But I should. Like ripping off a Band-Aid.

"Can I come over?" the text says.

That's not what I was expecting.

"Um. Sure," I write back, even though I'm not sure at all.

Even though I feel like I'm falling into a trap that I'm too dumb to even recognize.

The doorbell rings almost immediately, and I'm completely confused because technically Ruby should be in gym class right now and not at my front door.

I open it up, not even checking my hair or anything. I know how terrible I look. No reason to hide it. I haven't showered since Saturday. It just feels like nothing matters anymore. Who do I even have to impress?

"You need to read this," she says, shoving a navy-blue binder into my hands and walking through the front door, sliding her shoes off like she owns the place.

"Did you text me from outside?" I ask.

"No, I was next door getting that binder."

I examine it like it has some kind of disease. "It's Gideon's."

"Yes. And you need to read what's in there."

"I would rather not read anything else about how awkward and pathetic I am. But thanks for thinking of me." I try to hand the binder back to her, but she waves it away and takes a seat on the couch.

"You need to read it, Kyle. I'm not joking. He's your best friend. He loves you."

"He really doesn't," I say, flopping into the easy chair and tossing the binder on the coffee table.

"What if I tell you he loves you so much he had to make a list about the things he doesn't like about you, just to talk himself out of it?"

"I'd say that he's brainwashed you, because he tried to tell me the same thing the other night, but I didn't believe him."

"Kyle, read these lists. Or else I'm going to read them out loud to you."

I definitely don't want to have to hear all the mean things read aloud by my ex-girlfriend, so I might as well get this over with.

I pick up the binder and flip to the first page. It's a to-do list, a very Gideon-like to-do list. The words swim a little, as they do thanks to my brain being broken. I can feel Ruby watching me.

"Could you maybe stop staring at me? It's not making any of this easier," I say.

"Yeah, sorry about that," she says, picking up a copy of *Weight Watchers* magazine from the coffee table.

Some of the lists are very logical. *Am I gay or just Kyle-sexual?* makes me laugh because it's so Gideon. Then another one is ways to hide his feelings for me, followed by a list of reasons we'll never work. Most of the things on that list are related to the fact that Gideon seemed to think back then that he wasn't my type. I especially like the part where he says he's like Danny DeVito to my Chris Evans.

Everything in this binder is basically the opposite of the terrible, horrible, no-good list. It's everything that makes me feel good about myself. It's everything that makes me remember why Gideon's my best friend.

Ruby is not-so-subtly watching me over the top of her magazine.

"Where's the bad list?" I ask, flipping back through the binder but not finding it.

"Apparently Gideon had a fit of guilt about it several weeks ago and burned it."

"Why did you text that list?" I ask her.

"In the interest of full disclosure, it wasn't me. But I shouldn't have taken pictures of it to begin with. I'm very sorry."

"This doesn't fix everything," I say.

"No, I know. But it seemed like something you should see."

I nod. "I think I need more time."

"Yeah, that makes sense. But I wanted to make sure you had a sense of the whole picture."

"Maybe I should keep this," I say.

"Sure, I don't think Gideon would mind."

"Did he know you were doing this?"

"I talked to him, but he didn't know where the binder was. Turns out Ezra had hidden it from him."

I roll my eyes and shake my head. "That's so Ezra."

"It is," she says, getting up to leave.

I walk her to the door. "Thanks, Ru."

"You're totally welcome."

twenty-five

Gideon

Kyle comes back to school the next day. He doesn't talk to me, but at least he's there. The good news is that slowly but surely other people start talking to me again. Ruby starts sitting with me at lunch, and as the week goes on Sawyer and Maddie come back, along with some other people from student council.

I find out that Ezra had the binder and that Ruby made sure Kyle got a chance to read it. But if there's anything I know about Kyle, it's that when something bothers him, more than anything he needs to be left alone to hide in a blanket burrito for a while. We were friends for a long time, until I ruined it by being an idiot.

The student council election is coming up soon, and I

totally assume I'll lose. But I have to hope people are more forgiving than I expect them to be.

School kind of sucks without Kyle to talk to; I miss him a lot. I know I should probably try one more time to talk to him, but I don't want to rush him. Maybe he'll get so bored one day this summer that he'll just hop the fence and come sit on the deck with me out of nowhere.

That would be ideal.

I'm just really sad that we're not going to do everything we planned. Like we were going to go to Great Adventure over Memorial Day weekend and the Junior Dance a couple of weeks later. I hate that none of that is going to happen now.

The day before student council elections, I get home from school late. Really, really late, because I wanted to wallpaper the whole school with my slogan and posters. My parents are out for dinner and Ezra is sitting in the dark in the family room, watching *Teen Mom*.

"Hey Giddyup. There's something on the deck for you," he says.

"Like what?" I ask, glancing outside into the falling darkness.

"I don't know. Go look," he says, staring zombielike at the TV. He has a date with Ruby this weekend, and I'm trying not to think about how weird that is.

When I go out onto the deck, my navy-blue binder is sitting on the table. I know it's mine because there's a star on the cover that I drew with a silver Sharpie. I open the cover but I can't really see anything, so I wave my hands around to make the motion-sensor light go on. Then I sit down to read.

I've had this for a couple of weeks and I've made some edits to it. I hope you like it and you understand my vision. And my handwriting. God, I have terrible handwriting.

My smile cannot be contained. It's been almost two weeks since I communicated more than a brief "hi" to Kyle in the halls, and it's so relieving to hear from him, even if it's only a little note.

Every page after that has Kyle's messy scrawl on it, crossing things out and making funny asides.

The last page is a list written by Kyle. I get the feeling he's been working on it for a while, off and on, because a lot of the items are written in different-colored inks.

Things Most People Might Not Appreciate about Gideon, but I Do:

1. He writes terrible lists about people sometimes, but he means well.
2. He's short but fits perfectly in the crook of my neck. Also, he could still grow. Lots of guys grow even in college.
3. His hair is cute and curly even though some people might say it looks like a sponge. Maybe a sea sponge, because they're adorable.
4. He enjoys a good Disney movie. He enjoys bad Disney movies, too.
5. He uses big words, but I never have to be nervous about asking what they mean.
6. He knows when to back off and just let me be alone for a little while.

As I finish reading the list, there's the unmistakable sound of Kyle hopping over the fence behind me and I stand up to face him.

He has his hands in his pockets, but I notice for the first time in a long time he's not hunching his shoulders, as if for once he doesn't care if anyone notices just how tall he is. He leans against the deck railing while I stay by the table. I'm a little overwhelmed by his appearance.

"So, what do you think of those changes?" he asks.

"I like them. I think they work."

"Excellent." He smiles and takes a step toward me.

"So we can be friends again?"

He opens and closes his mouth.

"Or not. We don't have to be anything. I don't want to pressure you."

"No, it's not that," he says, shaking his head and taking another step toward me, this one longer and more confident. But he keeps his eyes locked on the deck floorboards. "I don't want to be friends anymore. I kind of liked the whole not-being-friends thing."

"Oh," I say, not getting it yet.

"I like the boyfriend thing. I think we were pretty good at that," he says, lifting his eyes toward mine and smiling.

"Oh," I repeat, feeling my shoulders deflate in relief. "I liked that thing, too."

"I'm sorry it took me so long to get here."

"No way. I'm sorry that I wrote any of that. And I'm sorry you had to see it and I'm sorry—"

He cuts me off by closing the distance between us and

pressing his mouth to mine. I lose track of everything and anything I was about to say. Nothing even matters except for his lips on mine. I fist my hands in his T-shirt and have no clue how long this even goes on, except it's long enough that the motion-sensor light turns off.

We both pull back and laugh.

"I wish there were lightning bugs," I say, looking out into the yard. "When was the last time you caught a lightning bug?"

"It feels like about a million years ago. Even if it was actually more like middle school." He puts his arm around my waist.

"They're so easy to catch," I say, leaning my head on his shoulder.

"You were always such a pain about them. You'd never let me capture them and keep them in my room. You'd make us release them at the end of the night."

"And then sometimes Ezra would hit them with a baseball bat."

"You should have just let us keep them safe in jars! So many lightning bug lives would have been spared," Kyle says.

"I wasn't that logical as a child. I just was kind of creeped out by the idea of them living inside. I could swear that I would hear them light up, and it scared me."

"I always kind of loved that about you. That you weren't very logical. You still aren't always very logical."

"For the record, I am a very logical person," I say.

"Sure you are," Kyle says, nodding.

"There's lots of stuff I love about you."

"Oh man, I didn't know this was a competition," he says, letting go of me and shaking out his arms like we're about to wrestle or something. "I was not informed that we were bringing out the big guns."

"Oh, I can bring out the big guns," I say.

"Let's hear it then. Big guns, go," Kyle says.

"I love that you just turned this conversation into a competition." Our faces get closer and closer with each sentiment, like we're playing a game of kissing chicken, but it doesn't matter because we're both going to win in the end.

"I love that you know when to ask if I need help."

"I love that you edited my Kyle notebook," I say.

"I love how you read ridiculously long books and then recommend them to me even though you know I'll never touch them."

"I just want to share good literature with you!"

"I love that you—" Kyle starts.

I cut him off by planting a loud kiss on his lips, which throws him into a fit of giggles and he nearly trips over his own feet.

"I love that you did that," he says.

"Well, yeah. Apparently we both love lots of stuff."

"Seems like it," he says with a shrug before pulling me in for a longer, deeper kiss.

I guess that's how it's going to be with Kyle and me from now on.

Acknowledgments

Thank you, as always, to the Swoon Reads staff. As a whole, you never fail to give me the warm fuzzies. Particular thanks to Jean Feiwel, Kathryn Little, and Caitlyn Sweeny. And of course to Nicole Banholzer for all of her excellent "publicist-ing."

Big, big thank-yous to the Trifecta of Awesome, Holly West, Lauren Scobell, and Emily Settle for being there at the inception of this book. To Holly for telling me about her ideal YA novel, Lauren for pulling us into her office to watch the video, and Emily for having random knowledge about high school basketball camp at the moment I needed it most.

To Lauren Velella, who always finds the time to read every draft (unless it's October) and always answers the phone when I need to babble. To Shayla Flournoy for reading this story while it was still in flux but for loving these boys anyway. To Rachel Schaffer for spending a long Saturday afternoon explaining Passover to me via e-mail.

Last, but never least, thank you to my family for their unwavering support. I would have never made it this far without them.

Turn the page for some

Sw♥♥♥nworthy

Extras...

Humans That Kyle Kaminsky
Finds Attractive

(Yeah, we'll start with the humans and save the inanimate objects for a separate list.) (I am not attracted to inanimate objects.)

1. Chris Evans (Obvious. I expect more creativity in the rest of the list.) (YOU'RE THE ONE WHO WROTE HIM IN. He just happened to be the first male person I found attractive.)

2. Elijah Wood (Now you're simply kissing my ass.) (Ignoring you.)

3. Demi Lovato (Makes sense. She's aesthetically pleasing.) (Thanks.)

4. Ben Savage (Because he reminds me of Gideon.)

5. Gideon (Because he reminds you of Ben Savage.) (Stop taking over my list. We'll do a list for you next.)

7. Alia Shawkat (Because she also reminds me of Gideon.) (I feel like she'd be offended by that on the off chance she ever met me. And if you told her she reminded you of me.) (Whatever.)

8. Ruby *(Still?)* (If this is a list of people I find attractive, then yes. I still think she's attractive.) *(Fair enough.)*

9. Harry Styles ~~(Kyle. NO.)~~ (KYLE. YES. You can cross him out all you want. I'll make him every name on the rest of this list.)

10. Harry Styles

11. Harry Styles *(Terrible.)* (Could be worse.) *(Do I even want to know?)* (Could be Justin Bieber.)

People Gideon Berko Finds Attractive

1. Kyle

2. Kyle

3. Kyle

4. Kyle

5. Kyle

6. Kyle

7. Kyle

8. Kyle

9. Kyle

10. That guy from One Direction who is cuter than Harry Styles. (No such thing.) (YES SUCH THING. The other one. You know, Larry.) (There is no Larry.) (They talk about Larry on the Internet all the time.) (Who is this "they"? There's Liam, Louis, Niall, and Harry. Zayn left the group.) (WHY DO YOU KNOW SO MUCH ABOUT ONE DIRECTION?) (Because I am a human with ears and emotions. And I have two younger sisters.) (You're sure there's not a Larry?) (YES.)

A Coffee Date

with author Sandy Hall and her editor, Holly West

"Getting to Know You (a Little More!)"

Holly West (HW): What is your favorite childhood memory?
Sandy Hall (SH): I'm number three out of four kids and my older brother and sister were nine and eleven when I was born, so anytime they were around was the BEST TIME EVER. Like, no offense to my younger brother, Sean, but when Karen and Scott came on trips or on family outings, it always felt like way more fun.

HW: When you were a kid, what did you want to be when you grew up?
SH: I got glasses when I was in first grade and basically wanted to be an optometrist for the next five years. Until I found out you had to go to medical school.

HW: What's your favorite scene from Lord of the Rings (or _The Hobbit_)?
SH: I'm a really big fan of the Smeagol scene at the beginning of _Return of the King_. I hadn't read the books before seeing the movies (I can hear all the Tolkien fans groaning in the distance. I AM SORRY!), so this was super-interesting backstory. And an unexpectedly light moment in what was going to be a dark movie. At least until Smeagol killed his friend.

HW: Gideon and Kyle are such huge Lord of the Rings fans that they learned how to write Elvish. What is the oddest/coolest/ most involved thing you've ever done for a fandom?
SH: I just did a little math, and I have something like half a million words of fanfiction floating around on the Internet. Definitely the most involved thing.

Swoon Reads

HW: What has been your favorite thing about being a Swoon Reads author?

SH: I love watching the process for the other authors. It's sort of an interesting position, because sometimes I know things before they happen and sometimes I don't. But I love keeping up with all of them on social media and seeing how things are going for them.

HW: This is your third Swoon Reads novel. Have you got the process down now, or is it different every time?

SH: It's a funny thing, but my process has definitely been different for each book and it continues to change. Writing *A Little Something Different* felt completely different than *Signs Point to Yes*, which felt completely different than *Been Here All Along*. I keep finding new and better ways to plan and write. I do a little of this and a little of that these days. I don't think I'll ever find the magical formula to writing a book, and that's probably a good thing. It keeps me guessing.

HW: What question do you get asked the most by your fans?

SH: Most of the questions I get are still *A Little Something Different* related because that's the one more people have read. I love when people ask if it's okay to like Victor. They're always so ashamed of their love for him. But I totally understand. He's the guy you love to hate.

"The Writing Life (Goes Ever On)"

HW: Where did you get the inspiration for *Been Here All Along*?

SH: It 100 percent came from you. And I guess Taylor Swift, since she gave the world that catchy little tune "You Belong with Me." I was totally into it once you laid out your idea, and I couldn't stop thinking about it for a month or two before I got around to planning it. But without your suggestions, it wouldn't exist.

HW: Well, I'm SO glad that you took my idea and ran with it! What's your favorite part of the writing process?

SH: PLANNING. I could plan forever, just listening to the new characters roll around in my head and start talking to me and each other. I love imagining scenarios and figuring out where they should go in the book. I love the actual writing, too, but that's more of a challenge and more about technique. The creative part for me really happens in the planning stages, and I love it.

HW: Got any advice you want to share with other authors?

SH: READ. I'm one of the worst offenders when it comes to keeping up with my TBR pile. I have a lot of trouble reading for pleasure while I'm in the middle of writing or editing. I end up going a month without picking up a book. And when I do, I remember how much I love reading. Authors really do need to make time for it.

Discussion Questions

1. Over the course of the story, Kyle learns that he has dyslexia and Gideon realizes he's gay. How do you think these new discoveries change how they view themselves positively or negatively?

2. If, like Ezra, you decided to skip college right after high school, where would you go and what would you do?

3. Gideon decides to get drunk at Maddie's party and come out to his friends. Do you think that's a good idea? What advice would you give him?

4. As best friends, Gideon knew a lot of good and bad things about Kyle. Do you think Gideon's mean list about Kyle was fair? Why or why not?

5. Who do you think is the most reliable point-of-view narrator and why?

6. Why did Kyle wait so long to come out to Ruby? Was it fair of her to get so upset?

7. After the list comes out, Ruby decides she wants to start taking more responsibility for her actions. In the end, who do you think was most responsible for the list getting published? How would you react if you were in this situation?

8. Have you ever felt as jealous of someone as Ruby felt about Gideon? Did you sympathize with her in any way?

9. When Kyle broke up with Ruby, she told him that she was going to tell everyone that she broke up with him instead. Why do you think image played such an important role in Ruby's life?

10. All of the point-of-view narrators in this story are hiding something at some point. (Gideon's gay, Kyle's failing English, Ruby's family has financial problems, and Ezra ran out of money.) Why do you think it was so difficult for them to share their secrets?

SWOONING FOR SANDY HALL?

Don't miss her other swoonworthy novels:

A Little Something Different

*Fourteen viewpoints.
One love story.*

The creative writing teacher, the delivery guy, the local Starbucks barista, his best friend, her roommate, and the squirrel in the park all have one thing in common—they believe that Gabe and Lea should get together.

Signs Point to Yes

The most adorkable romance ever!

When a superstitious fangirl's emergency babysitting job puts her in awkward proximity to her new crush, a nerdy-hot lifeguard with problems of his own, even her Magic 8 ball can't predict the turn their summer will take.

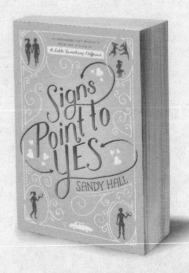

A romantic European vacation
is the perfect excuse to let go.

Nathan has never been one to play it safe, except when it comes to love.

No Holding Back

KATE EVANGELISTA

EVERYONE KNOWS THAT Nathan is in love with his best friend, Preston . . . everyone except Preston. Will Nathan find the courage to speak up, or will he lose his chance at love with the best friend he's ever had?

One

NATHAN WAS RIGHT where he wanted to be—hands clasped and biting down on the tips of his thumbs in a futile attempt at settling the tendrils of nerves coiling in his stomach. Maybe at the moment it didn't seem like he wanted to be where he was, considering his legs bobbed as he sat among the multitude of family and friends cheering on loved ones currently competing for a coveted spot in the Bennett Club. But yes, he was right where he *needed* to be—aging ten years in a matter of minutes. He wouldn't be surprised if he walked out of that facility with gray at his temples. God forbid.

The prestigious, privately owned swimming club in Colorado that Preston was trying out for boasted of producing the best of the best. Any kid who dreamed of being a champion swimmer dreamed of being coached by Bobby Bennett. Banners suspended along the walls of the gigantic state-of-the-art facility featured twenty-foot pictures of past Olympians—medals and fists raised in triumph. They were undeniable proof of results.

His gaze slipped to the empty seat next to him, where his sister Natasha would have sat had she not made some lame excuse for not coming along. In fact, they all should have been there cheering Preston on. But Caleb had classes at Loyola he couldn't miss.

Nathan sighed. He could still remember the absolute determination on Preston's face when the invite had been delivered via special courier. The envelope came a couple of days after his cousin canceled their European adventure to sweep Didi—now his girlfriend—off her feet. Only about a hundred were given out every year. And only a handful of swimmers were actually chosen. It was akin to finding the golden ticket wrapped around a chocolate bar. Preston hadn't even finished reading the letter before he had dropped everything and started packing.

For years one of Nathan's favorite things to do—besides planning magnificent parties—was watch Preston swim. It was like watching performance art. The way his arms sliced through the water, each stroke pulling him forward with speed and precision. The way his back muscles flexed took Nathan's breath away every time. It must be the closest someone could get to the perfect balance between physicality, endurance, and concentration.

Well, maybe not right this instant, since the swimming god was completely botching things.

"What the hell are you doing?" Nathan yelled, jumping to his feet and shoving his fingers through his dark brown hair—a Parker trait he shared with his twin sister and cousin. If strands happened to separate from his scalp from pulling too hard, he didn't care.

His shoulders tensed when Preston finished third in the hundred-meter freestyle. He removed his goggles and swimming cap in one smooth pull. Panting, he looked up at the digital board displaying lap times.

Even from afar Nathan could feel the frustration radiating off his friend. To qualify for Team USA, a swimmer had to finish at least second in his respective event. Anything less was unacceptable.

Time for an ass-kicking.

To say Preston ate, slept, and breathed swimming was an understatement. It wasn't even a stretch to say he devoted every waking moment to the sport. As soon as he was old enough to figure out how to hold his breath underwater, he'd been a swimmer. He knew nothing else. Didn't want to do anything else. Watching Michael Phelps bring home seven gold medals in a single Olympics set his benchmark. His ultimate goal.

And what a complete loser he'd been all day.

Beyond frustrated, Preston slapped his hands on the pool's edge and heaved himself up. He hadn't always been this wobbly in the water. Coming in third? He couldn't even remember the last time that had happened. He should have been kicking their asses. There were only a few heats left. If he didn't make something happen soon, he could kiss joining Coach Bennett's team good-bye.

Sure, he might still be able to train elsewhere in preparation for the Olympic Trials in June next year, but it wouldn't be the same. Being part of the Bennett Club would give him the edge he needed. It was already the end of August. Many of the other private clubs were full, and he'd said no to all the collegiate team coaches for this, his best chance at becoming an Olympian—and he was sucking spectacularly. Maybe he should have kept his options open.

Fuck.

He snorted into the towel thrown at him by one of the staff. As far as he was concerned, Coach Bennett was it. The dream coach. If he couldn't make it into the Bennett Club, then what else was there for him?

Nothing.

"What the hell do you think you're doing?"

He lifted his face from the towel to stare into the blazing blue eyes of the one person unafraid to call him out on his shit. At five foot ten, Nathan was in full battle mode.

"I just can't seem to gain my stride," Preston said, irritation at himself leaking into his words.

"Of course not," Nathan said. "You're too in your head about this."

Preston slanted a glance over to the silver-haired man in a blue jacket watching the swimmers with a keen eye and a stern expression. "I thought maybe . . ."

The slap on his chest forced him to return his gaze to Nathan. In a lime-green sweater and white slacks, he stood out among the men and women strutting around in tight Speedos. Yet something about the confidence in his stance made him fit in anywhere.

"Don't think about Bennett. No one cares about him."

Um, maybe I do? Preston thought.

But maybe that was it? That he cared way too much?

"Nate—"

"No!" Nathan interrupted, wagging his finger. "I don't want to hear any more excuses from you. I'm fed up seeing you lose."

"But—"

Nathan crossed his arms and cocked his hip to the side, displaying his best I-don't-give-a-damn-what-other-people-think stare. "We did not fly all the way to Colorado just so you could choke at the very last second. Third? Seriously? When was the last time you placed third in any race?"

"Then what do you think I should do?" Preston asked, heat creeping into his tone.

Nathan rolled his eyes as if the answer was obvious. "Maybe calm the fuck down?"

It dawned on Preston all at once. "I'm a fucking idiot."

"Exactly! Stop thinking too much about Bennett and focus all your energy on swimming." This time the slap against his chest was one of reassurance. "It's what you're best at. Stick with the butterfly for now."

"But those aren't until later."

The butterfly was the most challenging stroke, so the fly heats were always slated for last. Competitive swimmers had to be proficient in all styles, but everyone had a favorite stroke. Preston just so happened to possess the shoulder strength and the arm span that made him lethal at the one he enjoyed most.

Nathan tilted his head. "Better for you to rest up. How many heats are there?"

Preston did the mental count. "There's the hundred-meter and the two-hundred-meter."

Nathan's eyes grew saucer wide, as if he suddenly understood something he might not have at the beginning. "The freestyle has six heats, while the butterfly usually only has two. Somehow you got it in your head that being in the water more will show Coach Bennett what you're made of."

The last part sounded more like a question, but Preston knew it wasn't. "Maybe."

"Pres, you are one of the best swimmers I know."

"I'm the only swimmer you know."

"You can't afford to suck any more than you already have," Nathan said. "You're making me look bad."

Preston kept his expression blank, but inside he was wincing. Maybe even dying a little. But not from the obvious joke at the end of Nathan's words. He knew just how much he was sucking. The truth hurt like a punch in the gut.

Showboating. That was what he had been doing. Sure, he could deny it all he wanted, but it didn't mean it wasn't the truth. He wanted to be top dog. Unfortunately, he'd bitten off more than he could chew. Damn it all to hell.

"Switch gears," Nathan continued. "Show Bennett and everyone in this building why I flew a thousand miles just to watch you swim."

The corner of Preston's eye twitched. "Of course you're making this about you."

"Hell yes, this is about me." Nathan shot him one of his better grins. The kind that hid nothing from the world. "Don't embarrass me out there, Pres. Show them what you're really made of."

Preston snorted.

Nathan's features softened. "You're too stiff. Remember, just have fun. I know this is your dream. I know it might feel like the world is over if you don't get onto this team, but if you don't have fun, then it wouldn't be worth it either way. Trust your training. Breathe and loosen up."

And just like that, Nathan turned Preston's humiliation into renewed purpose. His fingers closed tightly around the towel he'd been holding. He faced the fifty-meter pool currently filled with his competitors. Somewhere along the way he'd let his nerves get the better of him when he should have been concentrating on what he did best.

"The bastards won't know what hit them," he said, meaning every word.

"That's what I like to hear." Nathan turned on his heel. As a parting shot, while walking away with a strut like only he knew how, he said over his shoulder, "Give them hell, Pres. Give them hell."

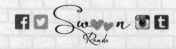

© Susana Ramirez

SANDY HALL is the author of *A Little Something Different* and *Signs Point to Yes*. She is a teen librarian from New Jersey, where she was born and raised, and has a BA in Communication and a Master of Library and Information Science from Rutgers University. When she isn't writing or teen librarian–ing, she enjoys reading, marathoning TV shows, and taking long scrolls through Tumblr.

sandywrites.tumblr.com